Meet me in Kasane

By the same author

THE SHRINK
HOPE

KASANE

BRIGITTA ZWANI

Biggles & Boggles.

Cover Designer: Book Cover Zone
Printer: Fujian Juhui Printing Co.,LTD
Edited by Cecilia Gathoni
Proofreading by Philip Odhiambo
Typesetting by Toonsday

ISBN : 978-99968-62-86-1
eISBN : 978-99968-62-88-5

To Botswana's hidden wonder

ACKNOWLEDGEMENTS

It takes a village to raise a child, in my case my children are my books. Kasane had a large team of friends that helped raise it to what it is now. I would like to extend my thanks to a number of people. Cobus Calitz thank you for hosting Paige and I at Qorokwe camp in the Okavango. The staff was amazing, warm, hospitable and went over and beyond to make us comfortable. Bigani Setume, it was a pleasure meeting you, thank you for believing in me and opening a few doors that helped with my research for the book. We fought, we laughed, we had sleepless nights, but all in all it was worth it. Thank you so much for being my fact-checker and pushing me to my limit.

To the owners of Peter's Place, thank you for allowing me to name my lofts after your beautiful BnB. Snuggled in the far corner of Phase Four in Gaborone, your enchanting BnB has been my home away from home for many years now. I am grateful for the hospitality you have extended to me. It is reassuring to know that I always have lodgings in Gaborone every time I visit.

To my Beta Reader, thank you for our priceless contribution to elevating the quality of my story.

To my family, immediate and extended, thank you for your un-ending support.

Enjoy xoxo

Brigitta Zavan

Rice

"DON'T STIR THE RICE WHEN COOKING IT, that's what makes it sticky."

"What? Are you talking to me?" Tori said, raising a quizzical brow.

"Yes, I am. I called you, didn't I."

Tori removed her cell phone from her ear, looked at the screen to double-check if she was indeed talking to Mpho. "Are you okay?"

Tori heard Mpho exhale. "I am fine. I'm just a little ticked off by my neighbour."

"Oh?"

"Yah, you know how she always wants to stick her finger in every pudding."

"You mean pie," Tori giggled.

"You know what I mean, stop teasing."

"So, when do you get here?"

"Change of plans. I am going to have to meet you in Maun. Something came up that I can't put off."

"Oooookay… So I am to drive alone to Maun?"

"Put some music on and enjoy the ride."

"Mpho. This is supposed to be a girl's trip. Emphasis on the sssssss… if you're not with me, what's the point of this?"

"What do you want me to do? Hubby says he can't get off early, which means I must wait for him to knock off, and then I take off. I can't leave Bella home alone."

"What happened to your maid?"

"She is off this week. She had to travel back to Zim for a funeral."

"Rats!" Tori's head was racing.

"What?"

"You know I have a bad knee, I thought we would take one car and you could drive part of the way, and then I take over, instead of me driving the whole way."

"I know. Why don't you break your journey ko Gweta? You could spend the night. We are being picked up on Thursday at eleven in the morning, which is plenty of time for you to drive to Maun from Gweta."

"Okay, sounds like a plan. But I really would have loved for you to have been on the trip all the way."

"Sorry tsalu. Such is life. One day you will get married and have kids, and then you will understand."

Tori shook her head, "Me? Married, with kids? I think not."

"It can happen."

"Mpho, I have tried to find Mr. Right, and the men that have always been interested in me are Mr. Impossible, Mr. Irresponsible, Mr. Unreliable, and the list goes on."

"I know, but I still have hope that Mr. Right is out there for you, Tori. And we will find him."

"Please don't bring your matchmaking hat with you on this trip. I just want to have a good time with my friend and not worry that she is trying to hook me up at every chance she gets."

"I can't promise." Mpho giggled on the other end of the line.

"Let me finish making something to eat, I will be leaving in about an hour. I should be in Gweta around four this afternoon or so."

"You didn't stir the rice akere?"

"No, I didn't."

"And?"

"Let me check." Tori took off the lid from the pot of rice. Using a fork, she gently grazed at it.

"Well?" Mpho prodded.

"It's fluffy." Tori smiled.

"There, see?"

"I never knew that. My rice has always been sticky. I thought you had to stir it to stop it from sticking at the bottom."

"Noooo… you just pour in water, salt, and a bit of butter, then leave it to be… check it now and then, but never stir it. The result? Fluffy rice."

"Thanks, let me finish cooking. So, we will meet in Maun then?"

"Yes. I will take the Orapa road, I hear the Nata-Maun Road is bad. Which route are you taking?"

"I am sticking to the devil I know. The Nata route. At least I know where the road is bad. And will take your suggestion and stopover in Gweta."

"Most of that road is bad, I don't know what you mean by 'where it is bad'."

"Not all of it is bad… just parts."

"Okay Tori, I'll meet you in Maun, at around 10 a.m. I'll have to travel really early so I don't miss the ride to the camp."

"Mmmm, see you then. I'll message you when I get to Gweta."

"Sure."

The drive to Gweta was uneventful. Tori had hoped to see a few wild animals. What she did see, however, was evidence of elephants. There were a few dismembered trees just before Sowa Pan, and ellie droppings here and there. Other than that, the only wild animals she saw were the ones on the signposts cautioning drivers.

Planet Baobab was her destination, it was marked by a huge pink anteater on the right and a giant structure with what Tori assumed was planet earth. She slowed down and slopped to the left. The dirt road had clear markings leading her to the lodge. A big black gate was pulled open by a wrinkled man. He smiled and waved. Tori waved back while bobbing her head. Four vehicles were parked just outside the reception area. A grey Jeep, two Toyota Hilux Surfs; one navy blue and the other ruby red, and the fourth a white Prado that was covered in dirt. Tori disembarked and found her way to the reception. A well-mannered gentleman smiled at her.

"Good afternoon. My name is Charles, how can I assist you?"

"Hi, I am Tori, I haven't booked, but I was hoping to spend the night here. Maun is rather far, just thought to break my journey and carry on tomorrow morning."

"Yah? Where are you travelling from?"

"Francistown."

"Well, that's not too far."

"No, but I have a bad knee, and it acts up when I am on the road for too long."

"Mhm," the man nodded. He typed on the computer in front of him and smiled. "Room five is available. Here are the keys. Dinner is served at seven p.m. You can either order now, what you would like to have, or later. It's up to you."

Tori nodded.

"You can drive your vehicle around closer to the chalets if you like."

"Thank you. Where is your loo?" Tori enquired as she grabbed the room keys from the charcoal-coloured man.

"Just behind here," he pointed, "go round through the bar area. You will see the signs."

Tori hobbled along the path that she had been directed to go on. She stopped for a second to massage her knee before continuing her quest to find the loo.

The place was quaint. The bar area had old pictures of what Tori assumed to be old Bechuanaland. There was a chandelier made of beer bottles. Enchanting was the word for it. From the loo, Tori walked up to the barman who happened to be deaf. Fortunately for Tori she had been learning sign language for the past year. She strung along a few signs, and the man furnished her with a cool glass of merlot. Tori took a long sip before walking around the premises. The pool was glorious. The baobab trees, spectacular. They stood majestic, unmovable, like ancient sentinels. As Tori made her way on one of the paths that led to the rooms, she scanned each chalet looking for number five. Finally, she spotted it hidden behind a magnificent baobab that looked to be thousands of years old. Upon opening her temporary abode, she couldn't help but smile. She knew this trip was going to be good. She was enveloped by a feeling of serenity. She felt content and the dry red merlot was doing a wonderful job of relaxing her bones.

Tori decided she would drive around to her room after dinner. She walked back to the lapa, and asked Fredrick, whose name she kept missing even after a couple of slow finger signs on Fredrick's side and instead simply signed to him by his sign name, the letter 'F' on his chest. She then ordered a burger and fries. The internet was dodgy, it kept fluctuating with the wind. Tori had paid a hundred pula for one device, something she had never heard of.

"Paying for one device," she mumbled under her breath as she typed in the password. So, if she wanted to use her laptop, she would need to get another password for that device. "Ridiculous!"

she muttered.

"Arrived alive," she typed and sent the message to Mpho.

"Great, I am just packing now. Will leave maybe at four a.m, or perhaps three a.m."

"Yah, you should make it on time for the eleven o'clock pick up tomorrow. Be careful when you get to this side, the wild animals."

"Yah. I need to be careful the whole way actually, cows on the southern end, and elephants up north."

"Lol!"

"See you soon."

"Sure."

The evening was uneventful. Tori enjoyed her meal after which she ordered a chocolate mousse for dessert. Her glass was refilled again before she walked to the fire that was being generously fed with the logs of dead Mopane trees.

"How come you are alone?"

Tori tilted her head and found herself looking into the emerald green eyes of a Caucasian stranger. "I…I…am…"

"Sorry, my name is Gabe." He held out a hand.

Tori obliged. "I am Tori." She gulped. "Nnnn…nice to meet you."

"Nice to meet you too. So? Why are you alone?" he prodded.

"Urm, well. I wouldn't say I am alone. I am travelling to Maun and will be meeting a girlfriend of mine there."

"But you are alone here?"

"Yes," Tori answered hesitantly. The man was being impertinent, she thought. What business did he have asking her why she was alone? "And you, why are you alone?" she poked.

"Oh," he smiled. "I work in Maun, just went for some medicals in Francistown, thought to break my journey here. It's one of my favourite spots."

"Oh," Tori nodded. Impertinence was something she was not familiar with and was not about to start cultivating the trait now.

"Okay, it was nice chatting with you, I need to sleep early, I am flying tomorrow." The man spoke to Tori as though they were old-time friends.

Tori creased her forehead and nodded.

Her thoughts drifted to the last time she was on the road to Maun. It was when she was still schooling at Delta Pine. Some memories were vivid, others blurry. She remembered the journey to Maun with her parents... Her thoughts were interrupted by Fredrick, who came to ask if she wanted more wine. Tori shook her head and continued to gaze at the fire before her. The flames were dying down, it was close to ten at night, and there was thunder rumbling in the distance. Tori slowly got up, walked to her car, drove round to her room, and removed her luggage.

The next morning she woke up with a stiff neck. "I must have slept funny," she mumbled. She took a quick shower and made her way to the lapa for some breakfast. Coffee was on demand.

"Most of our guests left early for the morning drive, so we didn't bother making a buffet breakfast."

"Oh?" Tori raised an eyebrow at the caretaker.

"Yes madam, so if you like we can make you an English breakfast?"

"No, that won't be necessary," Tori nodded as she added sugar to her coffee. "I will just finish my coffee, settle the bill and be on my way."

"Very good ma'am."

By the time Tori was back on the A3 it was eight-thirty. She had to be at Maun Lodge at eleven a.m for the pickup. The last time she spoke to Mpho, she was in Rakops. The possibility of them arriving at the same time was very high. Tori kept a minimum speed of 120 km per hour.

It was ten-thirty a.m when she pulled up at the parking lot at Maun Lodge. The GPS had done a good job of not getting her lost.

She was warmly received by the staff at Maun Lodge. Tori and Mpho had made prior arrangements with the lodge to leave their cars for a few days while they explored the Delta. Tshepo was the lady that had been assigned to assist.

"Good morning, Miss Amin? We hope you had a pleasant trip?"

"Yes, it's Tori Amin. My trip wasn't too bad, thank you. I broke off in Gweta, that helped."

"You are spending two nights here, correct?"

"Yes, but not right away. We are going into the Delta today, but when we get back, we will be spending two nights here."

"Okay," the lady moved behind the counter and punched a few letters on the keyboard before giving Tori a placid smile. "Your vehicles are staying, correct?"

"Yes, ma'am. Will that be a problem?"

"No," Tshepo shook her head, "they will be safe here. You will be in the Delta for how many days?"

"Three nights."

"Okay, so you will be here on Sunday?"

"Correct."

"Okay, your room will be ready for you, just pop into the reception to collect your key."

"Thank you."

As Tori was signing a few forms for her car, she caught sight of Mpho by the corner of her eye. "Just on time," she smiled.

"Shoo.. that drive was brutal."

"I can imagine!"

The friends hugged before kissing each other on the cheeks.

"How was your trip?" Mpho asked, exhausted as she removed her light grey pashmina, a thick, soft scarf with tassels.

"It was okay, the stopover ko Gweta really helped. Especially with my knee."

"Did it give you any issues?"

"Yah, when I arrived in Gweta. I think with the road being the way it is, I was moving my foot between the brakes and the gas frequently so that constant movement affected my knee."

"Well, at least for the next couple of days you will not be driving. Mmmm, speaking of which, I believe that must be our ride."

Tori looked in the direction of Mpho's eyes. An eight-seater safari jeep parked next to Mpho's car.

"Okay, ladies," Tshepo interjected. "Please follow Tumelo, he will show you where to park your vehicles. We will see you in a few days. Enjoy your travels."

Mpho and Tori walked outside and introduced themselves to the man in the safari jeep that was branded Qorokwe.

"Morning, I am Mpho."

"Tori."

"Nice to meet you both, I am Sizo. I will be driving you to camp."

"Lovely!" Mpho beamed, the fatigue from the long drive had evaporated and was replaced by the excitement of spending a couple of days off the grid, in the Okavango Delta, one of the world's wonders. "We are just parking our cars and will be with you in a minute."

"Not a problem ma'am. Do you have any luggage that is going to camp?"

"Oh, yes," Mpho stopped in her tracks. We might as well remove our luggage here, neh."

Tori opened her car boot to remove her luggage. Mpho did the same. Sizo swiftly took hold of their belongings before stowing them neatly inside the jeep.

The ladies drove round to their designated parking slots. A few minutes later Sizo spotted them as they made their way back to the jeep. The ladies climbed aboard, making sure they were comfortable.

He turned towards Mpho and Tori. "As mentioned before, Sizo is my name. I will be driving you to camp. The drive will take about three hours. We will see several wild animals on our way there. So just hold tight and enjoy the ride. There are a few drinks and snacks, please help yourselves." As he spoke, he pointed to a cooler box that was between Tori's seat and Mpho's. There was a little storage area between them. Mpho opened it and found a little fleece folded in the storage nook. Tori helped herself to a Savanna Cider that was tucked among other beverages in a generous amount of ice.

Sizo ignited the metallic beast. It came to life and roared through the parking lot and onto the main road, navigating itself through the traffic till it made its way onto the road leading to Shorobe. The drive on the tarmac seemed to drag. But neither Mpho nor Tori seemed to mind. In fact, it looked like the pair were thoroughly enjoying every minute of their sojourn, a needed break from their day-to-day hustle in the big cities.

The vehicle suddenly took a sharp left turn into a dirt road. Sizo slowed down allowing the bumps that came with every curve to sit gently on Mpho and Tori. The area was dry. A few trees looked disheveled, as though despondent with life.

"Elephants!" Sizo's voice cut in. "They have done all the damage that you see around here. In the community, it is war between elephants and the residents. The elephants destroy all the crops and the trees, as you can see."

"But why do they do this to the trees?"

"For nutrients. Can you see how dry it is?"

Mpho and Tori nodded.

"Yah, so the elephants look for nutrients in the barks of the trees. In as much as we say they are destroying, they are trying to survive the dry season. Without the trees to feed on, where else would they find nutrients?"

Tori nodded, took a long gulp from her cider, and kept watching the landscape as it kept shifting, from Mopane trees to palm trees, to shrubs, and finally to long blond grass. They passed a number of bridges that were made from thick gum pools. As the metallic beast mounted on one of the bridges, Tori was convinced they were going to be toppled over. She raised an eyebrow at Mpho as the jeep dismounted the bridge. Mpho smiled and took a sip from the glass of red she was enjoying.

"We are close to the buffalo fence," Sizo announced.

"Oh?" Mpho prodded for more information.

"Yes. The buffalo fence is the fence that keeps the wild animals from the domestic ones."

Tori made a face that said, "Oh, I didn't know there were fences around."

"This is how we try to keep the lions, hyenas, and other predators from the people that live on the other side of the fence. The fences also help with disease control."

And sure enough, five minutes later, they were going through a gate with a notice board, the sign read Morutshe Veterinary Checkpoint, open six a.m to ten p.m. Soon after crossing the gate, wild animals could be spotted, from elephants to zebras. Impalas were scattered generously through the savanna grassland. There was a pool of water that housed several hippos. The metallic beast then came to a dead halt.

Sizo pointed, "Lion!"

A pride of lions lounging under a Marula tree. Six were under the Marula tree as Sizo drove closer. Two that had been out of sight were clearly seen lying at the base of a giant termite mound that looked as though it was swallowing an acacia tree whole. Mpho and Tori sat in awe!

"Can they see us?" Mpho asked.

"They can only see one giant object. Not us as individuals," Sizo smiled.

"Mhm." Tori nodded as she took her phone from her bag. She snapped a few shots, then sat in total awe. She had seen lions before but not as close as she was now. She turned to look at Mpho and noticed that she had also been awestruck. Sizo allowed the ladies to savor the moment for a few more minutes before he carried on with the journey.

"How far are we from camp?" Mpho asked.

"Two minutes. These tents here," Sizo pointed, "are staff housing."

"Oh, nice."

Sizo picked up his walkie-talkie and announced that the guests were a minute away.

The vehicle curved to the left. The camp was hidden among a cluster of indigenous trees. The woodwork had been designed in a way that made the camp blend in with its surroundings. As the vehicle came to a halt, there were three ladies who ceremoniously greeted Mpho and Tori. They waved their hands to and fro and gave Tori and Mpho a very warm welcome.

After being served a welcome drink and signing an indemnity form, Tori and Mpho were ushered to the dining room area.

"You have arrived just after lunch, but we saved something for you," the manager of the camp was saying.

Mpho and Tori smiled. Their chairs were pulled out, after

taking their seats they were tucked in, after which napkins were placed on their laps.

Mpho gave Tori a smile.

Tori responded by widening her eyes. She had never in her life been treated like a glass jar that was about to break. Waiters came with several dishes, placing them strategically on the table. Another waiter came with two bottles of water. "Sparkling or still?"

"Still, "Tori answered.

"And for you Mpho?"

Mpho's eyes widened, shocked that the waiter knew her name. "Sparkling please."

Once the waiter was out of sight, a lady in a chef's garb stood in front of them. "Good day, my name is Sadie. Today you will be having boti kebab with horseradish and tomato galette. You will also have lamb fried rice in the miniature traditional three-legged pots, and for salads, you will be having sundried tomatoes and red quinoa, citrus fruits, and olive and red wine beets. For your wines, you can choose if you would like to have the white or red Den Painted Wolf pinotage.

"The red wine will do, thank you," Mpho decided.

Tori leaned to Mpho, "I bet you they didn't stir the rice while cooking it," she giggled.

Qorokwe
Day 1

THE ROOM WAS GLORIOUS. Mpho and Tori had been put in room nine. The barman had walked them down the sandy trail leading to their room. It was a bit of a trek, which had made Tori a little uneasy. She once had a nasty encounter with a male baboon a couple of years back while on her lunch break in Gaborone. The primate had chased her down a deserted concrete road leading to Kgale Hill. Tori was not looking for another round of unpleasantness. She had also heard stories of predators walking around camps, surprising guests in their chalets. With each step, she felt her stomach churn. Once in the room, Tori could relax. The chalet sat on large wooden stilts that gave it the needed elevation for a perfect view of the lagoon. The room was spacious. A double bed was situated in the center of the room, with a mosquito net draped around it. Tori noticed that the material used to build the chalets was eco-friendly. Wood, steel, and canvas. All three elements used to accomplish the contemporary design of chic and elegance. The colours mirrored nature ever so perfectly. There was a cream sofa, single bamboo chair, a rattan stool, weaved baskets, terracotta pots with sun-dried wildflowers as decor. As the ladies explored the room, they found an en suite bathroom that housed a freestanding tub, his and hers vanities, and an indoor-outdoor shower. Mpho and Tori walked around in amazement. They could not believe that a place like this existed, tucked away in the Delta. Most of all, they could not believe they had been invited to spend the long weekend at this luxury camp.

"I can't believe your Mark hooked us up like this."

"I know. His job has perks."

"And my my, what a perk. This place is amazing!"

The ladies walked to the deck that overlooked the lagoon and bushveld. There were only impalas and warthogs on site.

"Urg, I wish there were hippos in the water. Such a shame," Tori exhaled.

"Mhm, kana the hippo is your favourite animal."

"Yah," Tori said as she leaned on the rail. "I just love the sounds they make. It always sounds like they are laughing at each other."

The barman who had escorted them to the room, stood by the large sliding door. "Excuse me ladies, I have completed inspecting the room. All is in order. Over here is where you can charge your devices." He walked to the side of the bed and showed Mpho the multi-plug adaptors and USB charging points. "The Wi-Fi is free. You can log on to room nine Wi-Fi. Here you have the horn, in case of an emergency, and you also have a flashlight and in case you need anything a walkie-talkie."

"Thank you," Tori heard Mpho say.

The man-made his way out of the chalet. "If you do not want to be disturbed, you can put this rope on the latch. That way you will not be disturbed."

"Thank you so much. Much appreciated."

"At three-thirty," the man carried on, "there is high tea. Would you like us to pick you up or would you like to walk to the main deck?"

"We will walk," Mpho smiled.

"Okay, your evening game drive will be at four p.m."

"Thank you, kindly."

After the barman was gone, Tori and Mpho sprawled onto the

large cream bean bag slouch chairs that were on the deck. Mpho took off her shoes and picked up her phone. "I better tell Mark we arrived safely lest he worries."

"Yah, good idea," Tori said with her eyes closed. "What time is it?"

"Three fifteen."

"Urg, so we only have like fifteen minutes before we have to go for high tea."

"Mhm." Mpho responded with a frown on her face.

"What is it?"

"My WhatsApp messages to Mark are not going through."

"Try the landline."

"We don't have a signal here remember."

"Oh, eish!"

"He should be home right now with Bella."

"Don't panic, he probably went out with her for a walk or something."

"Mark never takes Bella for walks."

"Mhm."

At three-thirty the ladies were back at the main area. They were presented with high tea which consisted of iced tea, coffee, and bush tea. Mpho and Tori nibbled at some of the finger foods while walking around the deck that overlooked the lagoon. There was an infinity pool just below, adjacent to a fire pit with camp chairs circling it.

"This is wonderful. Thank you for thinking of me."

"Nonsense, who else would I have come here with?"

"Your husband," Tori smiled.

"He said he was on call, so couldn't come."

"Mhm."

Sizo approached Mpho and Tori. "We are just waiting for two guests who have just arrived to freshen up. In the meantime, we can saddle up in the jeep."

"Okey dokey," Mpho said, springing to her feet.

"Did you manage to get a hold of Mark?"

"No, unfortunately not," Mpho sighed.

As the ladies neared the car, there were two gentlemen already in the back seats. "Those must be the guests we were waiting for," Tori mumbled.

"Why, that's Mark!" "What are you doing here?"Mpho screeched, rushing to Mark's side, "and where is Bella?"

Mark smiled. "Surprise!"

Mpho climbed into the jeep and made her way to where Mark was sitting. She leaned over and gave him a peck on the lips, before punching his arm. "Where is Bella?"

"I dropped her off at your mom's. Thought I'd surprise you. And this is Glen." Mark gestured to the man that was seated next to him. "He is my colleague, just transferred."

"Nice to meet you, Glen. I am Mpho. This silly man's wife. And that's my friend, Tori."

Tori raised her hand from where she was sitting. "Hi, Mark, lovely surprise. Mpho was stressed out earlier when her messages weren't going through to you."

Mark looked at his phone. "Yah, no signal. We flew in, so we had no signal. And we still don't have any signal."

"Yah, there is only Wi-Fi in our rooms," Mpho said, still standing next to her husband. Pleasantly surprised that her husband was right in front of her.

"Would you like to sit next to your hubby, Mpho?" Glen asked.

"Please!"

"Sure, no problem. I can move." Glen got up and climbed over the middle seats and ended up next to Tori on the seats just behind the driver.

"I am Tori."

"Glen."

"Nice to meet you."

"Okay," Sizo started, "we will be going on a game drive that will last about two hours. Please mind the branches on the drive, and if you see anything that I may miss please don't hesitate to stop me. If you have any questions, feel free to ask. I will try to answer you the best I can." Sizo slid into his seat and started the ignition. A few staff members were standing on deck, waving to the tourists as Sizo looped out of the camp area and headed east. A herd of elephants were the first sighting. The vehicle came to a halt. Tori snapped a few shots and so did Mark and Glen. "This is a herd of females with their calves. Usually, bulls forage on their own. They mix with the females during mating season. You see these trees, how they all look chopped to pieces. Elephants. They look for nutrients in the trees during the dry season. That female there is tuskless."

"Is it because of poaching?" Mpho asked from the back seat.

Sizo smiled, "no, it's genetics. Some elephants have no tusks. If it was poaching, she would be dead."

Mpho nodded.

"Look at that elephant, its tusks are backward," Glen pointed.

"Mmm, this is also genetic," Sizo said as he turned the ignition key and hit the gas. "I would like us to quickly head to the wild dog's den before dark. We have a few pups."

"So how do you know Mpho?" Glen turned his attention to Tori.

"Oh," Tori shifted. "We are childhood best friends. We grew up together in Phikwe."

"Is it?"

"Mmmm."

"And you know Mark from work, correct?"

"Yes. We are on the same team. This trip is actually work."

"Oh?" Tory prodded.

"Yah, there have been reports of animals that have been dropping dead for no reason at all, so we are visiting several camps to try and ascertain what the problem may be."

"Mhm. Could this have something to do with the herd of elephants that were found dead at a watering hole a couple of months back?"

"Yes actually."

"Wow. And you guys still haven't figured out what the issue is?"

"No. We thought it was poaching. But it isn't," Glen leaned over and whispered, "So, we are visiting different camps to investigate the water sources discreetly."

"Mhm," Tori nodded.

"Branches," Sizo's voice cut through the air. The couples quickly leaned into the vehicle. Sizo slowed down, and eventually put the vehicle on neutral. He picked up his binoculars and scanned the sky before resting his eyes on a tree that was covered in vultures. "Mmm, looks like there is a corpse over there." He put the jeep in first gear and rammed forward veering off the beaten path. The four by four climbed through dead trees and branches with ease. Sizo maneuvered his way through the thicket till he found the corpse. It was a giraffe.

"Puff," Mpho exhaled at the back.

"Mmm, this smell will attract the hyenas. Looks like the young male died of natural causes."

"How can you tell it's male," Tori questioned.

"See the horns. A female's horns are normally thin and tufted, whereas male giraffes have thicker horns that become bald at the top. And it is definitely death by natural causes because there are no bite marks. If it had been a lion, a leopard, or a cheetah, they would still be here feeding, and the jugular would be dismembered. But see, the neck is still intact."

"Wow."

"And here we have three types of vultures. We have the White Backed Vulture, the Hooded Vulture, and the Lappet-Faced Vulture. We also have the undertaker here; the Marabou stork."

"Oh wow, I didn't know that the Marabou feeds on carcasses," Mpho interjected.

"Yes. The Marabou stork is known as the undertaker in the animal kingdom because of its appearance, when seen from behind its back wings look cloak-like. You see," Sizo pointed, as a stork walked in the opposite direction, with its back to the vehicle. "It resembles the grim reaper." He laughed as he turned on the ignition and wiggled the jeep out from between the dead branches, logs, and shrubs. A few odd turns later Sizo stopped the safari vehicle. "There!" he pointed. There was a shrub, and a hole in the ground that looked like it belonged to an anteater. "See?"

At close inspection Tori noticed a few puppies sleeping under the shrub, perfectly camouflaged. As her eyes got adjusted to the patterns on the wild dogs, she managed to locate more of them in a nearby tree, near a termite mound, and yet others a few meters away under an acacia tree.

"The pups look like there are different age groups," Mark commented.

"Yes. It's unusual. Usually, a pack has an alpha male and an alpha female. The alpha female is the only one that mates with the alpha male. We don't know what happened here. It looks like three females got pregnant around the same time. The alpha male may have been confused."

The group nodded.

Sizo moved closer to the pack to give the tourists better shots of the dogs. "Have any of you seen wild dogs before?"

"No," Tori and Mpho chorused.

"They are gorgeous," Tori said, as she took a few shots on her phone.

Glen whipped up his Canon, zoomed in, and took a few shots of the dogs. Everyone sat in silence as they enjoyed watching the little pups playing. Suddenly there was a high-pitched squeal, and all the male dogs started to strut to and fro.

"That's the call from the alpha male, it's time for them to go hunting. One of the females will stay behind to take care of the pups, but it's hard work, cause the pups always want to follow the males to the hunt," Sizo said. Tori picked up that Sizo had a nasal tone to his voice and a slight lisp.

After the males had finally separated from the nursing pack, they strutted single file into the bush. Sizo followed them closely, till they disappeared into the thicket.

"That was amazing," Tori smiled.

"It sure was," Glen said as he looked at the shots he had taken. He leaned over to Tori to show her the shots. Clear and crisp.

"Do you like photography?" she asked.

"It's a hobby of mine. I love being in the wild. I guess that's why I'm interested in wildlife."

"Have you always loved wildlife?"

"I guess. As a child, I always had pets, not just one but several. I was also obsessed with worms."

"Worms?"

"Yah… I loved going fishing with my dad, so I would breed my own worms."

"Wow, I've never heard of worm breeding!"

"It's a lucrative business, especially if you live in an area where fishing is a thing."

"I guess Maun would be the best place to start a worm-breeding business." Tori teased.

Glen smiled back.

A high-pitched squeal came from the vehicle, "what is this, Sizo stuck," Sizo said as he put the vehicle into four-by-four gear, and then swerved the wheel from side to side before stepping on the gas heavily. The car moved slightly, then moved a bit more, eventually the sand gave way and released the jeep.

Sizo carried on with the tour, pointing at every antelope, giraffe, elephant, buffalo, hippo, and bird he laid eyes on. His knowledge was vast, his enthusiasm infectious, making the drive enjoyable. They finally arrived at a deserted waterhole. The sun was preparing to set. Sizo parked the vehicle and announced a break. "Sundowners, anyone?"

All four passengers agreed.

Sizo walked to the front of the vehicle, pulled out what looked like a portable table from the hood. He then walked to the back of the jeep, carried a basket full of goodies, and laid out a spread. There was sparkling wine, Amarula, a merlot, nuts, crackers, and biltong. He asked each passenger for their preference and generously filled each glass with their beverage of choice.

Tori stood near the waterhole, her right hand holding a cracker and a glass of merlot in her left. "This is glorious," she whispered.

"It is, isn't it," Mpho approached.

"Nice surprise?"

"Wonderful surprise."

"And now, sleeping arrangements?" Tori whispered.

"No no, don't worry. I will still be with you. The boys can share a chalet. I wouldn't do that to you."

"Thank you."

"He is cute though."

"Mmm, he isn't bad-looking. But like you promised…"

"Yes yes, I don't have my matchmaking hat with me. I left it in Gabs."

"Good."

The sundowners were just what the doctor ordered. There was something about sunsets in Botswana. The blood orange ball seemed to emit waves of pixie dust leaving onlookers mesmerized, enchanted by its glory. By the time the ladies walked back to the vehicle, it was dark. Sizo turned on the lights as well as his flashlight. He flashed through the shrubs as he drove down the path leading back to camp. Suddenly he came to a dead stop. "Leopard," he announced. The light from the flashlight followed the creature on its path. The wild cat walked stealthily next to the vehicle with no care in the world, then suddenly it came to a halt. It sat on its hind legs and eyed the vehicle. Everyone was awe-stricken. Silence enveloped the night as a bat swooped by. Sizo savored the moment for a few minutes before starting the vehicle again. His flashlight darted again in the night, resting on treetops, water surfaces, and shrubs.

By the time they disembarked the vehicle, it was seven-thirty.

Dinner was ready. All four guests made their way to the open restaurant. For dinner, they were served fennel-crusted braised beef, stir fry, mushroom, and white wine pork stew with creamy mashed potatoes.

Chobe

Tori and Mpho were woken up by a tap at the door at six a.m.

"Good morning? It's Sizo. This is your wake-up call."

"Okay," Mpho croaked in her sleep.

A few minutes later her phone rang. It was Mark on WhatsApp. "Hey?"

Tori could overhear the conversation, Mark sounded wide awake. "We need to leave camp."

"What?"

"Yah, there has been a report of a herd of buffalo dropping dead in Kasane. Similar to those elephants."

"But it's six in the morning," Mpho protested.

"Yah, Glen and I are going to have breakfast then we will be dropped off at the airstrip, there is a plane that will pick us up with our gear."

"What about Tori and I?"

"You will have to stay here and continue with your safari."

Mpho was now wide awake. "Oh, can't we accompany you?"

"You will be in the way," Mark said firmly. "Plus its work."

"Well, you came to Qorokwe for work and we were not in the way were we?"

"I guess," Mpho heard Mark exhale. "Okay then if Tori is okay with us hijacking your plans then it's okay. I'll let Glen know."

"Okay, let me talk to Tori. We will be coming down for breakfast soon."

"Sure, see you then."

At breakfast the four sat in silence for a few minutes, taking in the gravity of the situation they had at hand.

"We need to leave immediately. We need to get samples from the buffalo before the decay advances."

"Really, it affects your findings?" Tori asked.

"That's what happened with the elephants, by the time we got there, there was hardly anything to sample."

"Heh banna!" Mpho exclaimed.

"Yah, so we need to move fast," Glen said as he took a sip from his coffee.

"Does this mean we are checking out?" Mpho enquired.

"Unfortunately, we have to," Mark said. "We can come back once we have laid this mystery to rest."

"What time is the flight?" Tori asked, looking at the time on her phone.

"At eight-thirty. I spoke to the manager already as well as Sizo. He is taking us to the airstrip right after breakfast. So if you both haven't packed yet, you better go back to the chalets and get your luggage ready."

Tori and Mpho shoved down as much of the breakfast that was in front of them as quickly as they could chew, then made their way to their chalet to pack. When they stepped out of the room, Sizo was waiting for them in the safari car with Glen and Mark.

"Really sorry to cut the tour short Sizo," Mark apologized. "But this is an emergency. We will be back soon, and we will carry on from where we left off."

"Not a problem. The issue you are trying to solve affects us too, you need to figure out what is causing these deaths. I know for sure it can't be poachers. They don't kill for sport. And they normally target elephants and rhinos but now you say even the buffalos are affected. It must be a dietary thing. A plant maybe, or the water."

"But if it was water, wouldn't all the animals be affected?" Tori questioned.

"Mmm, this is what we need to find out in Kasane."

The runway was a strip of compact dirt that stretched for about 1200 meters. The plane was small and noisy, and the journey was bumpy, leaving Tori queasy upon landing in Kasane.

Kasane was different. The town seemed to house more wild animals than Maun. Warthogs roamed the streets like stray dogs. There were signs in designated spots marked, "elephant corridor."

Tori giggled. "I have never seen anything like this before."

"Yah, Kasane is something else," Glen said as he disembarked the plane. Man and beast try to live in harmony. But most times man gets in the way of the beasts and man finds himself on the front page of the Daily News.

"Mmm... that doesn't sound good," Mpho said, placing her bags into the Wildlife car that had been left at the airport at Mark's bidding.

"Yah. So, keep your eyes peeled, if you don't bother them, they won't bother you."

"Where are we staying?" Tori enquired as she and the rest of the crew piled themselves into the 2013 Toyota Yaris Hybrid.

"The Old House."

"Oh, sounds quaint," Mpho smiled as she buckled up.

As it so happened, The Old House was quaint. It sat on the banks of the Chobe, overlooking the river. There was a white handwritten sign, The Old House B&B over a navy-blue board with three stars after the last B. There were flower pots in every nook and cranny. An old teapot that homed an extravagant fern. The surroundings were lush and fertile. Mark and Glen walked in to sort out the booking and get the keys. Mpho and Tori on the other hand walked past the pool and followed the trail right down to the riverbank. There was a fence that blocked any brazen crocs or hippos from dawdling onto the property.

"So?" Mpho smirked.

Tori tilted her head. "So what?"

"Glen?"

"Mpho, you promised," Tori shook her head in disbelief.

"Yah, but Mark was telling me how Glen couldn't stop talking about you."

Tori's lip curled, as her forehead creased at the same time. "We only spent one day together. What was he jabbering about?"

"Clearly that one day was enough for him to be mesmerized."

"Really Mpho. I thought this trip was supposed to be a girl's trip. But here we are with your hubby and a total stranger that is on the precipice of professing his undying love to me." Tori looked disappointed.

"Aren't you enjoying your trip?"

"I am, and I am grateful. It's just that I had hoped it would be me and you. Mpho, I have had so many failed relationships that I don't want this to be another."

"Is that why you have your guard up so high?"

"I guess. I mean, I don't see Glen as anything else but just your husband's colleague."

"Mmmm."

"You know my past. You know all about the matchmaking shenanigans my mother put me through."

"Yah, I know."

"And I must confess, a part of me would love to have what you have, minus the child."

Mpho raised a brow.

"Don't get me wrong, I love Bella. But I don't see myself ever pregas."

"Mmm, well neither did I, but look where I am."

"I know, your story is clearly different from mine. I believe at this point in my life at this age, I must just succumb to the fact that I will become an old maid, 'always a bridesmaid, never the bride', and always the aunt and never the mother. This is my life. This trip was just supposed to be about me and you, Mpho."

"I'm sorry Tori. I didn't know that Mark would come and surprise us like this. And swoop us from one camp to another."

"It's okay, I don't mind, honestly I don't. I just don't want the pressure, that's all. It always resulted in disaster in the past, and I can't imagine it not ending the same now."

"I get it."

"Maybe what I am looking for is something organic."

"And you meeting Glen wasn't organic?"

Tori shrugged. "I don't know, maybe it's 'cause my mindset is elsewhere."

"And where is that?"

"Just on enjoying my time out in the bush with my BFF, and not worrying about my nagging aunt who keeps texting me fortnightly, instructing me to "make a child," Tori made a face.

Mpho chuckled. "You need to block your aunt. Like, for real."

"Love?" Mark's voice cut through the air. "Our rooms are ready."

Mpho smiled, "We will be there soon. Did you take out the luggage?"

"Yah."

"Mark, please tell me I have a room of my own." Tori shot Mark a look.

Mark frowned. "Of course you do. You and Glen, have single bedrooms, whereas Mpho and I have a double."

"Oh darling, could you please get us some wine?"

"Sure, I'll be with you in a sec." And he disappeared amidst the generously scattered flora that had been deliberately planted about the B n B.

Mpho then turned her attention to Tori. "Is it because Glen is black?"

Tori's frowned.

"Well, blackish," Mpho bobbed her head like an Indian.

"Come on Mpho, you know me better than that. I have dated all sorts."

"I know, but all sorts are not to your parents' liking."

"I know, eish, my mom is something else."

"Mmm, remember when you were in Uni, how she lined up all those brothers of Asian descent."

"How can I forget," Tori shook her head, as though shaking the memory out of her brain.

Just then Mark appeared with two glasses of dry red.

"Enjoy."

"Thanks, babe."

Once Mark had disappeared, Tori gave Mpho a longing look.

"What?" Mpho questioned after taking a sip from her glass.

"That is what I am looking for. Casual familiarity."

Mpho looked up, "What does that even mean?"

Tori shrugged her shoulders. "He is familiar with you, and though you two are familiar there is still that spark. You still treasure each other. You can see that the fire is still burning even after so many years. He wants to make you happy, and you are attentive to him."

"Well, you can have that with Glen, if you would just let your guard down."

"Mmmm, I guess. But I just don't want to force things."

"Who is forcing… Come, let's go freshen up, and see what the boys wanna do." The ladies made their way back to the rooms. "Oh, are you cool staying a little longer than what we had anticipated?"

"Why?"

"Mmm, I have a feeling this mystery might take longer to solve than we both assumed."

"Yah, but our cars are in Maun, and we have booked. I guess we need to call and cancel the booking maybe?"

"I'll call and tell them we'll be longer than anticipated. And it's not like you are rushing back to work or anything, akere your last day at work was last week. Have you figured out what you would like to do yet?" Mpho gazed at her friend.

"Erm… not yet. Just thought I would enjoy this trip as I tried to figure stuff in my mind."

"Great."

"And wena what about Bella?"

"Ah, she will be fine. I'll check up on my mom and bring her up to speed with what is happening. It should be okay."

As the ladies walked past the pool, they gazed over to the restaurant and saw Glen and Mark having a couple of beers. The pair walked up to the gentlemen.

"So? What's what?" Mpho asked as she rubbed her husband's hair, before taking a seat.

"Well," Mark exhaled. "We have booked a chopper, so tomorrow morning Glen will scout things from up top and I will have my eyes on the ground."

"Can I join you on the flight?" Tori volunteered, resulting in Mpho's lip creasing into a lopsided smile.

Glen nodded.

"But," Tori asked shyly, "can we please find the pills that people normally take to stop one from getting nausea."

"Sure." Glen beamed.

Flying

THE NEXT MORNING, THE COUPLES were up early. They enjoyed a buffet at the restaurant before saddling up. The mission: to find out what was killing herds of wild animals. Tori was wearing a pair of olive-green shorts with white sneakers, a crisp white shirt - tucked, with rolled-up sleeves. Her corkscrew hair was brushed into a bun, her full lips painted in matt red lipstick. She had applied a little eyeliner and had brushed out her thick eyelashes with mascara.

"It doesn't hurt to try," Tori had said to her reflection in the mirror.

As they disembarked at the airport, Glen couldn't help but pass a compliment to Tori, which made Mpho and Mark smile.

There was a man standing next to a chopper that looked like an oversized dragonfly. As Tori and Glen approached him, Tori got the sense that she had met the man before.

"Good morning," the man smiled as he took hold of Glen's hand and gave it a good shake. "My name is Gabe."

"Glen,"

Gabe smiled and turned his attention to Tori. "And you are Tori," he winked as he shook Tori's hand.

Tori squinted, wondering where she had seen the man before.

"Gweta, you were alone, by the fire," Gabe assisted.

"Oh yes. You were traveling from Francistown, medicals, you

said."

"Right. Because I fly" he said, pointing at the chopper.

"Nice," Tori nodded.

"You are in Kasane now?"

"Yes, and so are you," Tori gently lashed back.

"I understand that you are in search of a herd of dead buffalo?"

"That is correct," Glen interjected, realizing that there was something there that he needed to put an end to, so he could stay in the running for Tori's attentiveness. "Mark and Mpho will be on the ground, I believe you will be in contact with the wildlife guy that will be driving them."

"That is correct," Gabe shifted a little, "so before we get on, has any one of you been on a chopper before."

"Sorry," Glen's face was perplexed. "Why are you flying us? Where is our guy from Wildlife?"

"There is something wrong with the chopper, and the guy that flies it called in sick, so here I am," Gabe explained.

"Mmmhm…" Glen didn't sound convinced. "To answer your question, I have been on a chopper before; I am not sure about Miss Amin here."

Tori shook her head, "No, can't say I have," she said giving a placid smile.

"Okay, a few safety tips. Please keep your seat belts on at all times. Steer clear of the back of the chopper, the rudders are pretty sharp. We will be flying at an altitude of ten thousand feet, once we reach the park I will fly lower. Should you spot something that I may have missed then please let me know and I will circle back. The headsets have microphones on them, so we will be able to communicate. Anyone prone to motion sickness?"

Glen pointed at Tori.

"A little, but I took some pills about half an hour ago."

"Okay great. I think we are all ready to rumble. Who would like to sit in front with me?"

Glen volunteered.

"Okay," Gabe walked to where Tori was strapped in and made sure her seatbelt was tightly secured. His masculine hands gently tugged at the belt, before giving Tori a wink. Tori noticed the freckles that were sprinkled on his button nose. The man had an effect on Tori that left her slightly dizzy. She noticed he hadn't shaved for a day or two, giving him a rugged, laid-back look. Gabe leaned back and dislodged the chopper's doors before placing them in a secure area. He then walked around, hopped on, put on his headsets before flipping a few knobs and punching some buttons. He mumbled something in his microphone and a metallic voice was heard responding. Tori couldn't make out any of the jabber, so she resorted to just laying back and enjoying the ride. The rotorcraft started to roar, as its wings cut through the air, Gabe took hold of the lever between him and Glen and proceeded to gently push it forward. The chopper took off.

"Where are you from?" Tori heard Glen ask Gabe.

"Austria."

"Wow, how did you get here then?"

"There was an advertisement. I had just finished my course, so I applied."

"How long have you been flying?"

"This is my first time," Gabe smiled. "No, I'm teasing. I have been flying for three years now."

"Wow! Do you enjoy being in Botswana?"

"Yes, very much so actually. I enjoy flying. You see something different all the time. Which keeps things exciting"

"I see."

"And you? Where are you from?"

"I am Motswana, from here."

"Really?"

"You don't think Batswana can look like I do?"

"Well," Gabe cleared his throat.

"My grandparents were from Zimbabwe. They moved to Botswana during the civil war years ago, and we were all born here."

"Ahhh. So, your parents are?"

"Coloured, yes, and my grandparents were coloured too. I am sure down the line there was a white person, who shacked up with a black person, but as far as I know, there have been generations and generations of coloured forefathers."

"Ahhh…"

Tori sat in silence, listening to the roar of the chopper as well as the uncomfortable chatter between Glen and Gabe. She suddenly caught something from the corner of her eye. "What was that?"

"What? Where?" Gabe asked.

"Just circle back. Under those trees. I thought I saw something."

Gabe swooped back to where Tori was pointing.

"Oh yah, that looks unusual."

There were two elephants swaying to and fro. On close observation, they saw another elephant laying on the ground. Gabe's voice was heard announcing a dead elephant to the ground team. He gave them the location before circling round again. It seemed to Tori that Gabe was looking for a place to land. He flew higher to try and get a better vantage point before heading three clicks north. Tori noticed a termite mound and a dried-up waterhole. The metallic dragonfly laid its feet on the ground before slowing down its wings. Gabe disembarked, followed by Glen.

Tori unhooked herself from the strong clutches of the seatbelt and followed the men out of the chopper. Suddenly there was a sound of a jeep approaching. Mpho and Mark were the passengers, with a pair of binoculars hanging from Mark's neck.

"Yah we saw the ellies just down there," Mark pointed.

"Hop on," the driver instructed.

"The trio jumped into the vehicle before it roared towards the direction Mark had pointed.

As they approached, they noticed that two more elephants had joined in the mourning ritual.

"How are you going to get past those giants to get to the deceased? Mpho enquired.

"Mmm, we can't really. We need to wait it out."

One of the bulls came from behind a tree, flapped its wings, and shook its head violently. Another rumbled nearby.

"I think we should leave," Tori suggested.

"Mmmm," the driver agreed as he turned on the ignition.

An elephant with a broken tusk blew its trumpet before charging at the jeep. The guide stepped on the gas and backed up quickly. "Hold on," he shouted.

The elephant ran after the vehicle for a good ten meters before stopping to flap its ears and blow its horn again.

"He did not look very happy," Gabe said.

"Yes, we will have to come back later once they are gone," the guide suggested.

"Did you guys not spot the buffalo yet?"

"No," Gabe said. Were you not given a clue as to where these buffaloes could be? If someone reported, surely they would know where the buffaloes are."

"Let me call base," the driver said.

Mpho and Tori gave each other looks. Silently saying, "How disorganized are these people."

The walkie talkie came to life. The driver asked where the buffaloes were located, and he was given a rough location. "I know where that is," Tori heard the driver say. We can all go in the jeep.

The driver from the wildlife department snaked through the bush, disregarding all the animals they came across. To him, this was not a game drive. It was a mission. And he needed to get to the buffalo as soon as possible. A few turns later they reached a cluster of dried-up shrubs. The smell was potent. The buffalo had started to decay.

The driver did a quick sweep, no predators were around. He nodded towards Glen and Mark, who quickly disembarked. Gabe was also on the ground keeping an eye on anything that moved. He walked further away from the car, tracking footprints. Tori's gaze fixated on him.

"He is cute," Mpho whispered.

Tori blushed and looked away. "I don't know what you are talking about."

"Tori, I know you better than anyone. From the time you got on that helicopter at the airport, it was as though the man had you under a spell."

"Lies," Tori said, trying to keep a straight face.

"Yes, lies. You are lying to yourself right now."

"Let's focus on the dead buffalo. How are they going to determine what killed the animals?"

"They need to run some tests."

"Is it?"

"Tori, you can admit you like him."

Tori's shoulders dropped. "He is really good looking, I'll give him that, but," she shrugged her shoulders, "that's about it."

Mpho laughed. "Why are you fighting it?"

"I know nothing about the man, except that this is the second time I am meeting him."

"When was the first?" Mpho sounded surprised.

"In Gweta."

"How come you didn't say anything?"

"There was nothing to tell. It was brief, he asked me why I was alone, and that was it."

"Really?"

"Yah, and he told me he just came back from having his medicals done 'coz he was flying.' What I didn't know was that he meant he is a pilot."

"You seem to know a lot about the guy."

"Glen was questioning him on our way here."

"Yah?"

"Mmm, I got the feeling he was threatened by him."

"Just a man-marking his territory," Mpho laughed.

After cutting open a few buffalo and examining their organs, collecting a few samples, snapping a few pictures, Glen and Mark stepped out of their overalls. Thabiso, the driver, and Gabe, had been patrolling the site, rifles in hand, while the ladies sat in the jeep at a safe distance.

Mark approached the jeep. "Babe please hand me that disposable bag."

Mpho obeyed.

After disposing of all the bloody gloves and overalls in the bag, Mark and Glen walked around the site, stern profiles plastered on their faces. Mark reached for his phone and made a few calls.

"Looks serious," Tori said, gazing at Mark.

"Mmmm, it seems to be."

"What do you think is the next step?"

"Take the samples for testing I guess."

"Mmmm."

The men all strutted to the four by four. Their work was done, and they needed to get the samples back to the lab as soon as possible.

"Is it safe to leave them here? What if some predator comes and eats it, won't they get what they got?" Mpho looked at her husband.

"Endoparasites die when the host dies. So, anything that eats them now won't be affected." Mark answered.

"Yah, worms of the intestines, liver, and those in the bloodstream are dead."

"So, what was the point of you taking samples then?" Tori asked.

"Standard procedure. There may be something that we will pick up. Rather do something than nothing, right?" Gabe added.

Mark jumped to the back of the vehicle and sat next to his wife. He placed the cooler box with the samples they had just collected into the storage compartment between their seats. "Yah, Ectoparasites such as fleas, lice, and ticks may die, but in many cases, they can also transfer to another host if one is available close by."

Gabe was still on high alert, looking for tracks to see if there had been any predators around. "Looks like none of them have found this pile yet."

"Mmmm, so what does this mean?" Tori tilted her head to look at Mark.

"Well, we are basically done here. We just need to take some samples of the water in this area. Thabiso here will drive us to the water holes nearby, and we will also take a sample of the water in the Chobe before heading back."

"Heading back?" Mpho asked. "I thought we were going to be here longer?"

"No. Our work is done. Glen and I need to double back to Gabs to get these samples looked at, as well as the samples we got in Maun. The sooner we can know what is killing these animals the better."

"Have you not had any of these incidents before?" Tori asked as the jeep parked near the chopper.

"No, actually, this is the first time we are dealing with something like this." Glen added.

Gabe jumped out of the chopper. "Anyone care to join me?"

No one volunteered.

"Okay then, I will see you guys when you see me," Gabe said before Thabiso reversed and made his way back into town.

"So that's it, your investigation is over?" Mpho sounded disappointed.

"We had an assignment, we have done what we needed to do, now we need to get these samples to the lab," Mark said as he pulled out his phone from his pocket.

"And the report will say there are no parasites because the animals are dead." Mpho persisted.

"Correct, but there could be something else that is killing the animals and not necessarily just a parasite." Glen smiled.

"I guess," Mpho frowned.

"So, when do you get back?" Tori asked.

"Erm, we could get the latest plane today?" Glen suggested.

"There are no planes going out today," Thabiso pointed out, "Only tomorrow morning."

"Okay, it will have to be tomorrow morning then," Glen said leaning in to avoid a branch that almost gouged his eye out.

"What about Tori and me?"

"The two of you can stay here for a day or two if you like or you can go back to Qorokwe," Mark suggested.

"Really love?"

"Yep." Mark said as he leaned over to kiss his wife on the forehead.

Tori looked at Mpho with a smile.

Kasane

Mpho and Tori were just from dropping off Glen and Mark at the airport.

"I don't understand. What does your husband do exactly? All these years I have known him to be in 'wildlife', but what exactly does he do?"

"He is an environmental consultant. He has explained time and time again what that all entails but I always forget," Mpho shrugged. "Why do you ask?"

"I am still thinking of the samples they took. Akere he was saying the parasites are dead, so what was the point?"

"I am sure there is more to the samples than he was letting on. They don't like to reveal information before they are sure of what they are dealing with. They are probably going to investigate what the buffaloes were grazing on and the like. I saw him looking at the shrubs and grass around where the buffaloes were, and they dug into the animal's intestines as well so they will find something, I am sure."

"Mmmm."

Mpho took a sip from the iced tea she was drinking, "Mmm, enough about all that, we still have a vacation to complete. Should we spend a day or two here?"

"Yah, that sounds like a great idea. And we are not too far from the falls. Did you bring your passport?"

"Yah, I did. Actually, I was thinking we may jump to Namibia since we were so close when we were in Maun."

"Do you mind if we went to the falls? I've never been."

"Of course, I don't mind. I think we should just notify Qorokwe as well as Maun lodge of our plans, akere we had booked to be at Maun Lodge, they will soon wonder what has happened to us, gape we hadn't finished our visit at Qorokwe."

"Good idea. We can go tomorrow, I guess. Wouldn't mind just chilling in Kasane and seeing what the place has to offer. I must say I am beginning to like it more than Maun."

"Really? Maun has more going for it."

"I don't know," Tori said as she signaled the waiter for another savanna dry. "I schooled there, remember?"

"Yah," Mpho's voice trailed as she tried to remember what the name of the school was.

"Delta Pine."

"Ehe, yes I remember you were boarding."

"Exactly."

"We should pass by the school when we are in Maun."

"Everything looks so different now. If I didn't have the GPS, I promise you I would have been lost coming into Maun, there have been so many developments."

"Ele gore what year were you at the school again?"

"Erm… let me think." Tori dumped more cider into her stomach as she tried to recall what year it was when she was at Delta. "I think it was around two thousand and three if not two thousand and two."

"Mmm."

"That school was full of misfits."

"Are you calling yourself a misfit Tori?" Mpho teased.

"You know what I mean. If I ever have a child, I would never send them to boarding school."

"Is that your way of telling me not to take Bella to boarding school?"

"Eh, I tell you, the mischief we got up to. We had a boarding master shem, she couldn't keep up with all the tomfoolery that was happening."

"To be honest I wouldn't want Bella to go to a boarding school either."

"Good. Kids basically raise themselves. Teen years are the most fragile years. It's a time when all your hormones are just going crazy and if not monitored and properly directed you can end up in a whole lot of problems."

"What problems did you get into?"

Tori smiled mischievously, "Wouldn't you like to know!"

"Tori, this is a part of your life where we have a gap in our friendship, you were doing you and I was doing me."

"Yah, I know, we were hardly in contact. You had just upped and left," Tori said rolling her eyes.

"Well, Debswana offered, what was I supposed to do, turn them down?"

"I know, I am just teasing. It was nice visiting you in Leeds that time."

"We do have some cool memories together."

"Yah, and I was such a jealous friend. Do you remember when we were young, you would make a friend and I would get soooo upset with you."

"Oh, do I remember?" Mpho laughed. "Our parents one time pulled us into a meeting and practically forced us to make up."

Tori giggled.

"What changed?" Mpho asked.

"I am still possessive. I've just toned it down a bit."

"A bit… mhm, is that your story?"

Tori chuckled.

"I am just thinking now, we should make a booking neh?"

"Yah, good idea," Tori signaled at the waiter again.

"Yes ma'am," The bald lanky man courteously approached Tori.

"We would like to book a few tours. Do you guys do that?"

"Yes ma'am, what would you like to do?"

"We would like to go to the falls tomorrow, and also go on an evening game boat cruise." Tori looked at Mpho for confirmation. Which she received in the form of a nod.

"Okay, what I can suggest is that you go to the falls on your own," he lowered his voice, "it's cheaper. And for the boat cruise, Dust till Dawn are the best. They have really nice boats, I would suggest the luxury cruise, it's a four-seater, and the service is," the waiter raised his right hand to his lips, making a sign of excellence.

"Okay, that sounds like a plan. So how do we get to the border?"

Mpho shook her head, "You know what, can we just get Dusk till Dawn to do everything for us, please. I don't want to start arguing with the money changers on the other side of the border, and then having to deal with taxi men that charge exorbitant prices."

"Okay," Tori nodded.

"So, you would like Dusk to take you to the falls?"

"If that is part of what they do." Mpho said, scratching her head.

"Okay, we can arrange that. I will make the booking, just the two of you mama?"

"Yes, so it's the falls in the morning, and in the evening do the boat cruise. Can that be done in one day?"

The waiter bobbed his head in thought. "Maybe break it down

into two days; the Falls tomorrow, and then the day after you can do the cruise?"

Tori cut in, "What are we doing this evening Mpho, why don't we do the cruise this evening, and then the falls in the morning, then fly back to Maun?"

"Sounds like we have ourselves a plan," Mpho smiled. "Are you able to sort that out?" she asked, looking at the waiter.

"So, you would like to do the cruise this evening, and then the Falls tomorrow?" he double-checked.

"Yes, please," the ladies said in unison.

The man sauntered to the office.

"Well then, at least we are sorted."

"Yah, it works out well."

"Lunch?" Tori asked.

"Sure, why not."

"I feel like a pizza, do you mind sharing it with me?"

"Yah, pizza sounds good."

The ladies enjoyed the rest of the day walking through the streets of Kasane. Tori was totally mesmerized by the town. "It's the warthogs,"

"What?"

"I think that's what makes this place what it is, the warthogs. Where else in Botswana do you get warthogs walking about in the streets as if they owned the place?"

"Well, technically they do own the place, people built in their habitat," Mpho pointed.

The ladies crossed the road as they made their way to the street vendors. They walked from stall to stall admiring all the arts and crafts that were on display. There were clay pots, carved animals, and others made of wire. Tori gravitated to the African-inspired earrings. She admired the craftsmanship and appreciated even more that the store owner was not following her around the stall as though she were a pick- pocketer waiting for a convenient moment. She picked up a unique pair of earrings. They were made from African print with hints of red, maroon, yellow, black, and gold, finishing the unique look. Tori held them towards the shop owner. "How much?"

"Hundred Pula."

"Wow," she started to place them down, then had a second thought to pay for them. "They are gorgeous," she said to the shop owner. The woman, who had a baby clinging to her like a baby koala, smiled, exposing a gap between her front teeth that were slightly discolored. "We will be back for the African print fabric," Tori promised.

Once Tori and Mpho were on the other side of the road, Mpho gave Tori a quizzical brow. "You are not one to throw money away like that."

"I know, but she spoke to me."

"What do you mean, she never said a word to you, she didn't even follow you around her stall."

"I know, but her eyes, Mpho. You can see the struggle she is going through to try and put food on the table for that wretched child of hers and I am sure that wretched child is not the only one she has." Tori's voice took on a different tone, "And I am not saying wretched in a derogatory way."

"No, I get you, you saw her. You did that thing you do."

"What do you mean?" Tori frowned.

"You wrote her story. You imagined her life."

"Yah," Tori's face slightly dropped.

The ladies walked into a little gift shop. A lady in her late fifties, if not early sixties was sitting behind the counter. She smiled as the ladies walked around the store.

"Are you visiting?" she inquired.

"Yes," Mpho answered.

"Kasane is a beautiful place. I moved here ten years ago. I was in Francistown. But originally from Zim, you know, when it was still called Rhodesia. The civil war sent us running." She chuckled dryly. The woman was an open book. Her mouth kept flapping as she dragged her shaking legs to where Mpho was standing. "I have always wanted to own a shop. It was either a gift shop or a café, you know, where you can have breakfast or lunch. Not the internet cafés you see around town. Those are not cafés."

Mpho smiled politely.

"This little tea set you are admiring was from my mother-in-law. She gave it to me on the day of my wedding. She was such a dear. My husband Gerald was her sweetheart. I could never do anything right." She said as she caressed the tea set. "Yah, Gerald never allowed me to use the set, he always said we would use it when his mother came around. His mother never came round," she croaked.

Tori blinked blankly at the postcard rack that was in front of her as she eavesdropped on the conversation. She moved to a shelf that housed an array of books.

The old lady caught Tori by the corner of her eye. "Oh, I love books," she hobbled to where Tori was standing. "I sit here all day reading. Well, not the ones you see on the shelves of course. I have stacks and stacks of books that I have collected over the years sitting at home. This is the one I am reading lately," she shuffled to the counter and came back with Chimamanda Ngozi Adichie's book in hand. "The Thing Around Your Neck. I just started reading it. I am determined to read only African authors. I am a great supporter." Her wrinkled pasty thumb flicked through the book. "Don't you just love the smell of books?"

Tori smiled sheepishly, "I don't think I have ever had the chance of smelling books, ma'am."

"Here," the woman shoved Chimamanda into Tori's nose and flicked the book with her crooked chalk-white thumb.

Tori's eyes popped, as she took a step back.

"So have you seen something you like?" the old lady asked as she eyed a JCB that was parked on the other side of the road. She walked closer to the window and shook her head. "You know, I always pray that that space you see there could be turned into something really nice. It is such an eyesore. You get men peeing there, or kids throwing rubbish. It's just a dump. If only someone could either buy it or just ask for that slot from the council and turn it into something tourists would be attracted to, it would bring joy to my heart. It burns my eyes just to look at that wasted space."

Mpho gave Tori a nudge. "We are supposed to be meeting the guide soon. Ma'am, thank you for showing us around your shop. It is very…" Mpho tried to look for the right word.

"Quaint," Tori assisted.

"Yes, quaint," she grinned.

"Well, you are always welcome to pop in whenever you want. You will always find me here. In my little corner, reading a book," she chortled.

Mpho pushed Tori out of the store, "We should make our way before we get late."

"Good idea," Tori nodded before following Mpho out of the gift store.

"What a bizarre conversation," Tori giggled.

"I know, she is pretty intense, shooo."

The ladies went across the road, past the open space the old lady had been complaining about.

"We should find our guide at the parking lot," Mpho said,

"dressed in the Dusk uniform."

"Did he say specifically where he will be?" Tori asked as she turned to look at the open lot again.

"I am not sure."

"Check your emails again," Tori said. "Maybe they were specific as to where exactly to look out for him."

Mpho went through her mail again, found the booking, and quickly scanned through it. "The tree next to the ATM."

"You mean that tree, and that ATM."

"Oh, great, that's him I guess."

The ladies approached the man with the Dusk till Dawn khaki garb.

"Hi, are you Gabriel?" Mpho enquired.

"Yes, Gabriel is my name."

"Great, this is Tori, and I am Mpho."

"Ehe! You are the guests for this evening's boat cruise. Welcome, welcome. I see the payment was done online. Wonderful, wonderful." The man was speaking to his tablet. He swiped it vigorously before he gave Mpho and Tori their full attention. "So, it is your first time on the Chobe?"

"For me yes, but Mpho has been before."

"Okay, so follow me please."

The trio weaved their way through the throng in the shopping mall and ended up on the other end near the riverbank.

"This is your boat," Gabriel pointed at the chic, cream-coloured luxury boat, with a glorious sign that read Dusk till Dawn. There were two other passengers already planted in two seats, leaving no options for Tori and Mpho to take the two that were vacant.

Gabriel went to the front of the boat, removed two life jackets, and handed them to Tori and Mpho. "If you feel you would like to put these on, please do. But you are perfectly safe in this boat."

"Tori?" A voice came from behind her.

She looked back to inspect who it was. After about a second it hit her. "Sebastian?"

"Yah, it's me."

"What are you doing here?" She gaped.

"I should be asking you the same question. The last we saw each other was where, Delta Pine?"

"That's right. I had just finished my A-Levels and you were still doing your form five."

"That's right, that's right," the man with dimples said, licking his lips.

Tori blushed, "oh, sorry, how rude. This is my friend Mpho," Tori pointed. "Mpho this is Sebastian, we schooled together at Delta Pine."

"Is that right," Mpho raised a disapproving brow. "Well, isn't this a small world?"

"It is," Tori said, trying to catch her breath.

Mpho gave her friend a quizzical look, which Tori tried to ignore.

"This is my friend Drew," Sebastian signaled to the man sitting next to him.

Gabriel's voice came from the wheel. "We will stop by the park office and register before carrying on with our tour." As he spoke, he wheeled the luxury boat to the park offices on the left side. He steered the boat close enough to the edge for him to jump out with a paper in hand.

"So where have you been hiding all these years?" Sebastian kept the conversation going.

"Well, here and there. I went to Uni in SA, then came back and started working."

"I kept up with you on Facebook, but then lost track of you."

"Bastian, were you stalking me," Tori teased.

The man gave off a confident laugh, "Nah, I wouldn't say stalking exactly." His voice was deliberately smooth, each word rolled off his tongue ever so gently. It was as though he had a speech impediment but at the same time didn't. Tori was totally taken in.

Mpho looked on at her friend in shock. Who was this man, she had never heard of Sebastian, in all the years she had known Tori. "Tsalu?" She tried reeling her friend back from cloud nine. Tori gazed at her friend for a split second before locking eyes again with Bastian.

"What have you been doing?" It was Tori asking.

Sebastian flicked his lips like a monitor lizard, "I completed my A-Levels at Delta Pine, then went to UB to do a course in Engineering."

"Oh?"

"Yah, I now work in Jwaneng."

"Oh, so that's where you are based?"

Gabriel charged on with his narration, "The bird you see hovering there is a kingfisher, he has spotted something, so he is looking for the right moment to make his catch," Gabriel's voice fell inaudibly onto Tori's ears.

"So, you are in Gabs?" Bastian asked.

"I was, for some time. My parents wanted me to go into the family business but I had other plans of my own, so I moved to Francistown."

"No wonder I have never bumped into you before."

"Yah, I guess. Our paths have been moving in two different

directions."

"Till today," Bastian continued.

"And you see over there," Gabriel pointed, "that is Sedudu Island."

"Are you going back to Francistown soon?" Bastian nudged Tori.

"Erm, I am not sure of my plans at the moment."

"Oh?"

"Yah, I just retired actually."

"Retired, at your age?"

"Yah. I don't like the seven to four working hours, so I wanna venture out on my own."

"Is that right? What do you want to do?"

"I am not sure yet."

Gabriel cut in again, "there was a dispute about the Island."

"Well, maybe you can come and visit me in Jwaneng, one of these days." Bastian suggested.

Mpho raised an eyebrow, "Tsalu, Savanna?"

"Sure, thanks."

Mpho popped the cider for her friend before shooting Sebastian a disapproving glare.

"As I was saying," Gabriel sternly said, trying to regain his audience. "That is Sedudu Island, there was a dispute……."

"So, you say Jwaneng?" Tori was thoughtful. "I have never been."

"Maybe it's the right time for you to come and have a look."

By the time the tour was over, Tori had not heard nor seen anything but Sebastian. Mpho was livid and the guide was unimpressed.

Kazungula Border

"WHAT WAS YOUR DEAL YESTERDAY?"

Tori shook her head, "I honestly don't know what happened. Something took over me and it was like I was in a trance. I haven't seen Sebastian in years."

"Mhm, well it looked like you were prepared to throw us over to the crocs and take away with him on the boat ."

"Don't make jokes."

"I am not, I am actually still pretty upset by the whole thing. I felt quite jilted. Did you even see anything on the boat cruise?"

Tori bit her lower lip.

"Exactly. You are not allowed to do this to me today."

"Promise," Tori said, putting up two fingers in the air.

Mpho rolled her eyes, "Whatever."

"What is your deal, aren't you the one that keeps saying I need a husband?"

"I don't think hooking up is what I want you to do. I would like for my good friend to find happiness."

"And what, Sebastian can't be that happiness?"

"Did you see that guy? He has one thing on his mind, as he kept licking his vile lips. I am sorry, I didn't like him, AT ALL!" Mpho stressed.

"Okay, okay. I get it. Honestly even way back then it was just physical attraction."

"So why are you pining over him now? You know nothing about the man. You guys looked like you picked up from back at Delta, you completely forgot that it's been years and that there may be things that you need to know about the man after so many years. What if a na le mogare? Or a na le bana, or a na le mosadi."

"Well."

"Exactly, men like him are pigs Tori. All I am saying is, be careful. Don't think an old flame is your safest bet. The flame didn't blossom for a reason. Let dead dogs die."

"It's let sleeping dogs lie."

"Whatever, you know what I mean."

Tori walked to the immigration officer, got her stamp, and walked out the exit. "I guess you are right."

"I know I am right. I have a radar for things like these."

The ladies climbed back on the safari car that was escorting them to the falls. They drove past throngs of people that were walking to the pontoon. As they approached the water, they saw a string of trucks waiting to be carried by the pontoon. One was approaching, carrying a group of men who Tori assumed were tourists. On closer inspection, as the giant raft got closer, Tori noticed that the men were fighting to be the first to jump off the metal float. As soon as they got close enough to jump off, there was a frenzy. The men charged at the people waiting on the pontoon on the Botswana side, demanding to exchange money, to carry their luggage, and even offering them lifts on their taxis. The men attempted to move to the safari car where Tori and Mpho were securely tucked in, but the driver gave them a dismissive wave.

The truck that had been on the pontoon disembarked, and another slugged its way onto the back of the metal float. A raven-black man in a cream shirt signaled for the safari jeep to approach. Tori and Mpho steadied themselves as the jeep climbed on. Those on foot climbed on before the pontoon started to crawl its way back to the Zambian post.

It was Tori's first experience on a pontoon. She had heard about it but never imagined that only two of these contraptions were being used to carry such loads, hourly and daily. The experience was tranquil. It was as though time had stood still. Things moved in slow motion. The clouds, the birds, the waters.

As soon as the float reached Zambian soil, all the passengers quickly disembarked, and the safari car followed suit. Gabriel parked the car next to an official-looking building. "This is immigration, let's get our stamps before continuing our journey."

The ladies obeyed. They followed Gabriel and lined up behind him, clutched their bags as they dislodged their passports from their pouches. Gabriel announced their destination and pointed to Mpho and Tori to inform the official behind the glass that he was travelling with them. The officer smiled, he found it unusual to see Dusk till Dawn on this side of the border. He was used to seeing the tour jeep on the Zim side. What he didn't know was that Dusk till Dawn had made an exception for the ladies, at Mpho's bidding the tour company had yielded. He signaled for the trio's passports before stamping day visas for them.

The jeep glided past the few officials standing at the border gate. One of the officers checked all three passports and nodded. Tori and Mpho smiled as they grabbed their passports from Gabriel.

"How far are the falls from here?" Tori asked.

"About an hour, give or take."

"But there is always a possibility to see some game on the way there, so just be on the lookout."

The jeep ambled its way through the pothole-infested tarred road. The scene was something out of a movie. As soon as you stepped into Zambia you noticed a distinct difference. Everything was different. The taxi's looked different, the people looked different, even their semauso's looked different. There was something chaotic about the place. The chaos seemed to work for the people and didn't seem to bother them one bit. Tori took it all in, her gaze shifting from one bizarre normal to another. There was a taxi on the side of the road and a man was busy pouring petrol into it.

Gabriel chuckled, "Street filling station."

The road to the falls was uneventful, there had been a police checkpoint on the way, but other than that, there was not much to see. Tori immediately noticed that the topography of Zambia was totally different from that of Botswana. The jeep slowed down as they approached civilization.

"Livingston," Gabriel announced.

"Oh, wow, so how far is Lusaka from here?" Tori enquired.

"About a four-hour drive."

"Wow, I thought it would be closer!"

Livingston looked like an old European town. It had the big homes and the type of buildings that had been built when the country was under colonization. Gabriel whizzed through the traffic, and eventually swerved to the right. The road was not too much of a stretch because fifteen minutes later they had arrived at their destination.

"Right, you can pay for your tickets. Then I'll drive you to the entrance."

The ladies did as they were told, and ten minutes later they stood in front of the entrance in anticipation to see the falls. Gabriel had parked the jeep next to a restaurant and had made himself comfortable at one of the tables.

Mpho led the way. Tori followed closely.

"Don't accept anything, nor agree to anything. There are some self-made guides in this place."

Tori nodded.

The ladies started off on the left. A thunderous sound could be heard just beyond the trees. Tori noticed that some of the tourists that were trekking back were soaked wet. She smiled politely as they crossed paths. Suddenly there was an opening, a gush of wind swept through Tori's straightened hair. She reached in her pocket for a scrunchy and tied it into a bun.

"Yah, neh, we are going to get wet."

"It's a good thing it's sunny today," Mpho smiled.

The falls were magnificent. The water cascaded on the rocks effortlessly. The gallons and gallons of water never stopped falling into the chasm.

"So, this is the water that comes from Angola?" Tori asked as she stood at the edge of the wall that prevented pedestrians from walking too close to the edge.

Mpho, who was standing at one of the information boards nodded. "Mmm, it is. The Zambezi is apparently the fourth largest river in Africa."

"Wow, which is the first? The Nile, maybe?"

"Yah, I should think so, Mpho said, as she approached the edge too."

The ladies were now soaked by the sprinkles. As you looked below at the gorge you noticed how painful and deadly a fall would be. Mpho pointed at the bridge. "Let's go to the other side."

The best friends spent the whole day walking through the grounds. They read most of the information that was placed at strategic points around the falls.

"Would you like to bungee jump?" Mpho asked as they looked at the adrenaline junkies on the other side jump from frightful heights into the unsympathetic gorge.

Tori's eyes popped, "No, no. I am fine with just walking around and looking. I saw they have helicopter rides, fishing, zip-lining, rafting, and, and, and. But I am happy with us just grabbing lunch at the really nice hotel we passed on our way here."

"The one where Gabriel is?" Mpho made a face.

"No. There is another one, much nicer." "

"Oh, you mean the Royal Livingstone."

"Yah, that one. Let's do that."

Gabriel was walking through the little craft stalls when the ladies exited the falls. As soon as he caught sight of his tourists, he marched to meet them.

"Gabriel, do you mind taking us to that nice hotel we saw on our way here?"

"Yes, sure. You can either walk through this back gate and you follow the walkway or I can drive you there."

"What do you prefer, Gabriel," Mpho asked, tilting her head.

"If you are comfortable walking and seeing the sites as you do, then I will find you at the lobby in about an hour or so?"

"Sounds like a plan," Tori smiled.

The ladies followed Gabriel's directions and walked through the back entrance of the lodge. The premises were gorgeous and well-kept. A wide range of tall trees provided the desired shading through the gardens. Mpho and Tori smiled as they followed the path to the restaurant.

The setup was authentic, the lounging open, chic, and classy. Tori smiled as they found their seats. The view was the Zambezi River, the weather was agreeable, and the staff eager. A waiter came to hand the ladies some menus.

"This place is amazing!" Tori said as her eyes took it all in.

"I know, neh."

"Is that a bride?" Tori's eyes were fixed on a Caucasian lady in a wedding dress. Just behind her, three women dressed in what seemed to be Grecian, nude coloured bridesmaid's dresses were carrying lanterns. A photographer was seen kneeling, tilting his head and camera in different angles.

When the time approached for them to pack up, Tori and Mpho were stuffed. They found a gift shop that was on the premises, bought a few souvenirs before finally mounting onto the jeep with Gabriel at the helm.

Qorokwe
Day II

Tori preferred Kasane to Maun, she realized it more when they were back at camp. Kasane was enchanting. Maybe it was the fact that Kasane was still wild. Instead of cows or donkeys walking the streets, in Kasane it was warthogs and impalas. The Delta though was paradise, there was something about being back in the bush. Cut from civilization, no messages were coming through; no WhatsApps, no notifications on Facebook, Instagram, or Twitter, just plain silence, unless you were in your chalet and had logged on to the wifi.

Mpho and Tori were warmly welcomed back and were assigned to room nine again. A day tour, an evening tour, and a mokoro ride on the river had been scheduled for them. The mokoro ride made Tori uncomfortable.

"You are sure that we won't get toppled over by a hippo?" she kept asking the guide.

"No ma'am, the water is too shallow for Hippo."

"And what about crocodiles?"

"There are no crocodiles on this river."

"How can you be sure about this?" Tori asked, suspecting that the guide was telling white lies to ease her nerves.

"We have not had any incidents ma'am, and we are confident we will not have any today. We have trained guides for the mokoro ride. This is Gopolang, and Mbiganyi."

"This is what confident people say just before a horrendous "incident," Tori said, making quotation marks in the air as she got off the jeep and followed the guide to the boats.

Both guides nodded at Mpho and Tori. They were both barefoot, dressed in Qorokwe camp uniforms. They smiled and ushered Mpho and Tori to their individual canoes. Tori stepped into the light-framed boat, as her eyes darted up and down the river in search of a rogue hippo or a blood-thirsty apex predator. She settled in the boat before Mbiganyi started to row the boat. He stood erect on the other end of the canoe, his feet perfectly balanced, while his hands gripped the long rod that he used to steer.

"So you say there are no hippos here?" Tori was at it again.

"Yes ma'am."

"But what if we come across a hippo that is trying to move from one part of the river to the next. What do we do then?"

"We won't encounter one."

"But how can you be so sure?"

Mpho's head tilted as they rowed past Tori and her guide. "Is she still grilling you on wild animals?" she asked Mbiganyi.

Both guides smiled.

"What was that? A rustling sound was heard beyond some water lilies, there were a few ripples on the water surface.

Mbiganyi smiled at Tori, "That is the river tide ma'am."

Mpho burst out laughing.

"You are laughing now Mpho, but this is how people die. You remember in the movie, Deep Blue Sea, LL Cool J survived because he was scared."

Mpho burst out laughing again. "There are no sharks here."

"No, but there are crocodiles, and anyways, who says there are no sharks. Haven't you seen documentaries on bull sharks? They are found everywhere. You never know."

Mpho was still laughing.

"This water is too shallow ma'am. If the boat capsized you would be able to stand in it."

"Tori, just lay back and try and enjoy this experience," Mpho giggled. "Look at the sun as it prepares itself to set."

"It's pretty."

"So focus on that."

"Fine."

The guides reached a cul-de-sac in the river and maneuvered the boats to double back to the safari car.

"How long have you been doing this?" Tori heard Mpho ask her guide.

"About three years," the man confessed.

"Do you enjoy this job?"

"Yes ma'am, it's different from other jobs. Each day your office is different."

"I like that," Tori interfered, "and you Mbi, how long have you been with the camp?"

"Just six months."

"Oh, wow! Did you study tourism?"

"No Ma'am, I only got to standard seven, then I did odd jobs here and there, till eventually, I was able to find work here."

"Oh, nice, and you went for training to be a guide?"

"Yes, you are taken for training."

Mpho's guide cut in, "Buffalo!"

Tori's eyes popped. There was a herd of buffalo on the river bank on the left. The scene was epic. The sun slightly touched the back of each buffalo as they bent down for a drink. Mpho looked on in awe as she pulled out her phone to take pictures. Mpho started to speak, "This…"

"Shhhhhhhh…" Tori's tone was shallow but stern. "Mbi, can

you row the mokoro away from these buffalo as fast as you can?"

The man obeyed.

To everyone, the scene was one to be savored. But to Tori, it was a scene one needed to escape, before being noticed by a psychotic testosterone-charged bull. Once out of sight, Tori started to relax a little.

"Tsalu, they were not going to do anything to us."

"Oh, so you spoke to them, did you? You asked them kindly, that they should go against their natural instincts of fight or flight, hm. You had that conversation?"

"Goodness! You should have taken a shot before getting on this boat ride," Mpho shook her head, a smile plastered on her face.

"Mbi, thank you for getting us out of there. I know this is your job and that you are not afraid of these wild animals."

"No, ma'am, I am afraid of these wild animals."

"What!" Tori was mortified. A wimp had been assigned to her. If they had been attacked he probably would have sacrificed her to the beasts and fled. "So how are you doing this work then?"

"Oh, I had wanted to do electricity. But the contract came with other jobs attached to it, and being a mokoro guide was one of them."

"So you are doing the job, yet you are petrified of animals!"

"I wouldn't call it petrified."

Tori got the sense that she had challenged Mbi's manhood.

"I would say I have a deep respect for wild animals."

"I like that Mbi. I like that a lot. See I also have a deep respect for them. If you don't bother them…"

"They won't bother you," Mbi smiled, finishing off Tori's sentence.

"I like you Mbi, you and I understand each other."

Mpho's boat had stopped alongside a cluster of reeds.

"Reed frog," Gopolang pointed.

"Where?" Tori squinted.

Mbi rowed closer. "There ma'am," he pointed.

"Oh wow!"

"It's beautiful neh," Mpho said, and she tried to get the right shot at the right angle.

"Yah, it resembles marble."

"Yes, this frog is common in the Okavango Delta," Gopolang continued. "Hyperolius marmoratus. This frog can be found in Malawi, Mozambique, Swaziland, Tanzania. The skin can be poisonous. The colouration and the patterns change between day and night. See now it looks sandy and pale. Perfect camouflage. You would just think it's a bump on the reed. But at night the colour changes." Gopolang rowed on.

"And these reeds? Is this lemongrass?" Tori enquired.

"It resembles lemongrass but it is not. And be careful not to rub your fingers on these reeds, because they will slice you."

"Mmm, and these lilies, is this where tswii comes from?" Mpho asked and she disembarked.

"Yes," Gopolang said as he pulled half of the boat out of the water.

The ladies found that Sizo had been waiting for them with a lovely spread. He smiled at Tori and handed her a glass of merlot, and for Mpho he handed her a glass of gin and tonic.

"How was the canoe ride?" Sizo asked as he walked back to the portable table to grab the bowl of snacks.

"It was excellent," Mpho smiled.

Gopolang and Mbiganyi smiled at the ladies and bid them farewell. Tori quickly reached in her handbag and gave the men a generous tip. "Thank you for putting up with me," she grinned.

"So you left your husbands in Kasane," Sizo asked.

"Mpho is the married one, I don't have a husband. Just silly old me," Tori took a sip from her balloon-shaped glass."

Sizo nodded.

"Do we know what is for dinner?" Mpho quickly changed the subject

"I am not sure. Our meals are quite varied." Sizo smiled.

"Ahhh, well whatever it is, I am looking forward to it. Any chance there will be a bonfire tonight?"

"Yes, actually, a very big chance," Sizo popped a few nuts into his wide gape and smiled.

There was a rustle behind a few bushes a stone throw away. Sizo walked towards the noise. Tori slowly backed up before cautiously climbing into the vehicle. Mpho gulped her gin and tonic and walked towards where Sizo was headed.

Tori watched on suspiciously as she shook her head. "Mpho, Mpho," she whispered.

Mpho gazed back.

"Get back here now," Tori gestured with a disapproving frown.

"Oh," they both heard Sizo behind the bush where the rustle had come from, "it's just warthogs."

Tori shook her head.

Back at the camp, the guests were served dinner on the patio. The platter consisted of goat shoulder pot, chicken arrabbiata rice pilaf, ratatouille, steamed baby marrow, cauliflower, poached pears, and bread rolls.

After dinner, the ladies walked to the fire pit. The flames flicked at the night sky like a hungry dragon. The ladies picked the camp chairs that were facing the lagoon. The sky was clear, a cloak of darkness.

There was chatter on the patio, more camp guests, Tori assumed. "This trip has been golden."

"Even though you were a hot mess this afternoon?" Mpho shook her head.

"I was, wasn't I? But it was a lovely ending to a beautiful day."

Bathusi, the bartender, was seen hovering near the patio stairs. Mpho gestured to him and he promptly approached.

"Is everything okay madam?"

"Do you mind if you could get me a glass of gin and tonic?"

"On the rocks?"

"Yes please."

"Very well madam, and for you Miss Tori?"

"I will have the merlot please."

"Very well. Coming up." And he quietly moved towards the bar.

"I thought that was you." A voice came from behind Tori and Mpho. The figure was not clear till the man moved closer to the fire. It was Gabe.

Tori smiled, "what are you doing here?"

"There were some guests here at the camp that had booked a flight over the delta."

"And they requested you?"

"It just so happened that I was on duty," he responded huskily.

"How are you doing Gabe," Mpho smiled on the other end of the fire, her smile was obscured, it blended into the dark night, and only bits of her teeth were visible.

"I am well thank you. Had dinner already?"

"Yes, the chefs here know what they are doing."

"Mmm."

The bartender arrived with the ladies' orders, served them then quietly made himself scarce.

"So you normally sleepover when the guests fly over the delta?"

"Oh, no," Gabe shook his head. "The chopper has a few technical issues that need to be looked at, so someone is coming over to check it out tomorrow morning. It would be dangerous for me to try and fly back to Maun."

"Mhm, that makes sense. Well, it's good to see you again."

"Did you guys solve the mystery of the Buffaloes?

"No, not yet," Mpho interjected.

"Such a shame and very random," Gabe shook his head. He picked up the glass mug that was next to him and took a gulp of its contents.

"So you say you are from where Gabe? Your accent seems a bit," Mpho shook her head and hand at the same time, as though to say, neither here nor there.

"Austria."

"Mhm, you love Botswana?"

"It's paradise!"

"Ao?" Mpho was shocked, "Austria, from what we have seen on The Sound of Music, is paradise."

"True, true, but that is a different kind. Botswana is a raw paradise. And flying over the Okavango is a privilege I can't get over."

"Is it?" Mpho gulped the rest of her drink and got up. "I think it's time for me to call it a night. I need to check on my little chicken and hubby before my eyelids clampdown."

"Do you need company?" Tori asked.

"No, no, I'll get the barman to walk me to the chalet."

"Okay, I'll see you."

After Mpho left, Tori and Gabe sat in silence for a few minutes, each one enjoying the company as well as the ambiance.

"So you are from here?" Gabe raised a quizzical brow, breaking the silence.

"Yes, born and bred."

"Really?"

"Why do you doubt?"

"I don't know. I think perhaps your looks?"

"What, just cause I don't have kinky hair, and a thick Motswana accent doesn't mean I am less Motswana than Mpho."

Gabe hid behind his drink. "How long have you and Mpho been friends?"?

"All my life."

"Why, it's nice to have friends like that!"

"True."

"So, I am sorry, and please don't scream blue murder for me asking. How come you look the way you do?"

The question pricked Tori more than usual. It's a question she had been asked all her life. Yet this time for some reason it pricked. She took a sip from her glass and cleared her throat. "Well my mother is Motswana, actually, and my father is Indian," she shrugged. "I am Motswana, I grew up here. Ke etse Setswana and I also know Tamil and English."

"Oh okay, wow!

How did your parents meet?"

"They went to school together. They did the same course, they fell in love and my two older siblings and I are the results."

"You have older siblings?"

"You are full of questions today, aren't you going to share anything about yourself?"

"You haven't asked me anything."

"Well, I haven't had the chance."

"Oh, sorry. What would you like to know?"

"Are you an only child?"

"No, I have one older sibling and one younger, both girls."

"Oh, so you are the only boy. Wow!"

"Yes."

"And your mom and dad?"

"I never knew my father, my mother is in Austria."

"Oh wow, what happened to him?"

"My siblings and I all have different fathers; my mother was a social butterfly in her younger years."

Tori regretted asking, she sat quietly, listening to the fire. Hippos could be heard laughing in the distance. The bartender hovered around again and then disappeared when no one called him over.

"Are you seeing anyone Tori?"

Tori choked on her drink. She coughed violently as she patted her chest.

"Sorry for asking so bluntly."

"No, it's fine," she squealed, her voice going funny as it tried to normalize. She took another sip from her glass. "No, I am currently not seeing anyone."

"If this is not too brazen, I would like to date you."

Tori's eyes popped.

"But you hardly know me."

"Isn't that the point of dating someone, that you eventually get to know them?"

"Can't we just be friends?"

"And all the time we are friends, am I supposed to pretend that I don't have feelings for you?"

"Feelings?" Tori choked again, this time on her saliva. After regaining her composure, she gazed straight at Gabe. "I don't know Gabe. I don't think it's a good idea."

"You don't trust me?"

"I don't know you well enough to trust you."

"But if we dated then you would know whether I am trustworthy or not."

Tori stood up and started to push the camp chair backward. "I think it's time for me to call it a night."

"It seems to me like you are running away."

"Well, I am not. I am just tired."

Gabe sat by the fire and watched as Tori darted out of the main area like she was being chased by a man-eater.

SIX MONTHS LATER…

Plateau

Tori parked the Surf full of her belongings in front of plot 2351. The land was bare, the ground hard, the plot empty and the possibilities plentiful. Plateau was a well sort-out area as it overlooked the vast Chobe. Tori exhales as she disembarked. She had been warned of wild animals roaming the town and had witnessed a few warthogs from her last couple of visits to Kasane after having enjoyed her vacay with Mpho. All she had seen on this drive were elephants and rusty remnants of car accidents. She had broken her journey at Elephant Sands and had enjoyed a night with Africa's gentle giants. There was something enchanting about the place. Maybe it was the fact that it embraced the outdoors. One was surrounded by nothing but the wild. It was a different environment from the city. There was less noise pollution, fewer worries, less technology, less stress. She took a couple of steps towards the edge of her newly purchased property. A lone acacia stood proud and sturdy. Tori approached it, sized it up and down before attempting to climb. She tried to navigate the thorns but found it impossible to ascend. Eventually, she gave up and decided it best to appreciate the view from the top of her van. She sat on the back of the metallic rose gold SUV, crossed her legs, and took in the view. It had been a long time coming, but eventually, she had made it.

After the girls' trip, Tori had enjoyed at Qorokwe, which had been conveniently disrupted by Mpho's husband and colleague, Tori had returned to Francistown with a strong desire to start a new chapter of her life. Life in Francistown was great. She enjoyed her independence. The slow pace. People in Francistown were not running or fighting… running in traffic to try and beat the time, running up the proverbial ladder to become the next big thing. Fighting to get into the latest hot spots. Fighting to have the biggest fan base. Fighting to be seen. Fighting for that "It" lifestyle. Francistown had a lovely slow pace to it. You could spend the day at work and then stop by Diggers Inn for a hot meal and a glass of wine without worrying that your hair was not tied in a perfect bun at the right angle. Or you could hang out in casual comfortable ripped and cuffed boyfriend jeans teamed with a tired striped t-shirt at the bowling club on a Thursday evening. Or you could knock off work early on a Friday and go and enjoy a game of golf at Pommies with friends. But it wasn't Kasane. Fine, Pommies had impala and a random peacock roaming around. But it just wasn't Kasane. There were no corridors for wild animals. There were no elephants chilling by Choppies, or crossing the path between the filling station and Nandos. And there were no warthogs.

It had taken Tori close to two months to wrap things up in Francistown, find a plot she liked in Kasane, and eventually, after a lot of chats with her parents who were based in Gaborone, make the move. Now, as she sat on top of her car, she couldn't help but smile. She found she was happy, happy at the prospect of a new life.

She was woken up by a rustling in the nearby bush. Dawn was breaking; the glow of the sun's rays was slowly piercing through the vegetation. Tori slowly peeled the blankets off. She raised the car seat and yawned. As she adjusted her eyes, she noticed a grey shadow floating past her window. Muffled thuds could be heard which Tori assumed were droppings falling to the ground, yet one could not hear the thumping of the Loxodonta. As Tori looked on in silence, it looked like their feet had been made of marshmallows. No sound. The mammals had mastered the art of stealth.

She brushed her teeth before wiping her face with some water from her water bottle. "Time to make some moves." Tori picked up her phone and dialed the number of the contractor she had been in contact with for the past couple of weeks. "Ten o'clock. Okay, no problem, I will be at the site, see you then."

The pot-bellied man arrived promptly at 10 a.m, plans in hand and a cigarette between his lips. He extended his stubby fingers towards Tori. "Stacy."

"Tori," she smiled as she wiggled her nose. Smoking was a vile trait she could not fathom. "So when do we start working?"

"As soon as you are ready ma'am, after the endless visits to council, the plans were finally approved. So when you say the word, I can get my men on-site and start erecting the structures."

"And you say the first loft will be done soon, around when do you suppose?" Tori jerked an interrogative eyebrow.

The man opened the plans, took a drag from his cigarette before exhaling the smoke from his funnel nostrils. "We were hoping to have the three buildings erected simultaneously. That way the project gets to be done quicker. My men are fast workers. The foundation is what usually takes a bit of time, and then the finishing. Erecting doesn't really take that much time."

"Oh," Tori thought ruefully. "I had hoped to stay on-site in my car while you built."

The man burst out laughing. It was a laugh that came from his belly. "Ma'am, we will have heavy machinery on site twenty-four seven. And from your timeline, we may be working through the night as well. I suggest you go find yourself cheap accommodation for the duration of this project."

Tori was thoughtful. Her naïve plans were already tearing at the seams. She felt a slight irritation ride up her spine. It was not because she could not stay on-site, but how the message had been delivered. The brusqueness of the heavy-footed man with a receding hairline and pants that could not accommodate his beer belly had left her fraught with anxiety. She had heard of how things mysteriously went missing on building sites. You would have bought five hundred bags of cement, but only end up with three hundred. You would order a truck to deliver ten tons of concrete. You would end up with only eight tons. She had hoped to be on site so she could monitor the building project. But now her plans were being thwarted.

"There are plenty of low-cost BHC houses that are up for rent. I am sure you can get one," the man suggested as he pulled his pants up.

Tori nodded. "I will have to do that," she responded drily.

"So when did you want the men to start working?"

"First thing tomorrow morning. I want them to work day and night. I am on my way to purchase flood lights, so you have sufficient lighting at night," Tori's voice was charged up. She was determined not to have her plans derailed. Nor was she planning on being swindled by a contractor.

Her first stop was at the BHC offices. She was ushered into an empty office. The officer in charge of allocating houses had stepped out. On one end there was a stack of files, and on the other, open aluminium filing cabinets that seemed to be vomiting their contents. There was a musky stench mixed with cheap coffee. A mug sat on the large wooden desk that housed an archaic cream-coloured computer. On close inspection, she noticed the sticky fingers on its body as well as a gummy keyboard next to it. Tori sat uncomfortably on a chair that matched the look and feel of the room. She tried to breathe through her nose but failed, so her mouth was slightly gapped.

"Sorry for keeping you waiting," a voice came from behind. A pudgy coffee-coloured lady walked into the room and shut the door behind her, leaving no ventilation in the stuffy sticky room they were in. "My name is Vicky," she smiled, exposing the gap between her teeth. "How can I help you, ma'am?

Tori gave a doleful smile. "My name is Tori Amin, I am new here in Kasane. I had hoped to live on my newly purchased site till the builders were done with my project, but they have kicked me off the site, and now I am basically homeless."

The lady on the other side of the mahogany desk took a sip of coffee, showing off her long, pink, almond, press-on nails. She shook her head as she placed the mug back near a cluster of ring stains that had marked the desk from countless coffee cups.

"So now I am in need of accommodation."

"Mhm, I see," Vicky nodded, as she slowly tapped the sticky keyboard with her fingertips. "Unfortunately, miss, there are currently no houses available. But I can put you on the list."

Tori's heart dropped. "On the list for how long."

"You see these files."

Tori followed Vicky's gaze and found herself looking at the stack of files.

"Those are all applications for houses. We have a two-year backlog."

Tori's stomach churned. She gave the plump lady a gracious smile, her brows flicked up and down before she pushed back the seat she was in. "Well, Vicky," she adjusted her bag. "Thank you for your time."

"So you don't want me to put you on the list?" Vicky enquired.

"No ma'am, that won't be necessary."

Tori's mind was racing as she jumped into her car and made her way to the hardware store. She picked up a few floodlights before heading to the site. As she drove around Plateau, she noticed many empty houses. "Backlog!" she sneered.

That night she slept in her Surf. When she woke up the next day, she had a stiff neck.

Peter's Place

Tori had been living in and out of her truck for the past six months. When she failed to get cheap accommodation through the Botswana Housing Corporation, she reasoned her situation would only be temporary. She had found an empty BHC house just around the corner from her site, parked her truck behind a crouched tree, and used the yard as her provisional abode. She knew no one in Kasane and the hotels were too expensive. Stacy had suggested she get a one room, or a two-bedroom house. After scouting around Tori had settled on living just around the corner in her car. She would be saving money she desperately needed. Plus, she was close to the site. Tori was always the first to arrive onsite and the last to pack up. In her car she had a five-liter container of clean water for drinking, brushing her teeth as well as freshening up. Each day around lunchtime she would drive to Cresta Mowana with her costume under whatever garb she had on. Made sure she was fully lathered with soap, so when she got to the pool she would take full advantage of it. The guard would smile, wave, and call her by name as she walked up to the lodge in her flops, summer shorts, and a Mary Poppins bag. A plate of fresh chips and an ice tea were her go-to before jumping into the pool. Some days were quiet and she would enjoy the pool to herself, making sure she scrubbed the bits that needed attention, and other days it would be packed, forcing her to do a quick discreet rub here and there before being caught out. After her dip, Tori would shimmy her way to the public toilet, pull out her toothpaste and toothbrush from her Mary Poppins bag, and give her teeth a good scrub. Next, she would pull out a bar of soap and spa bath gloves she had purchased at Woolies and give her face a good scrub. A few essentials would be tended to before she vacated the premises. This routine carried on for six months making sure she switched up lodges, so she could be 'missed.'

The construction of her lofts had taken a little longer than she had anticipated. For one, the steel that the quantity surveyor had ordered had been dear and hard to find. Eventually, Stacy had suggested a company in Zambia. This proved to be a blessing. Work was now taking shape. It was now August; Tori had hoped to have the lofts ready at least by October, so she could start getting bookings.

"How much longer Stacy?" She pushed as she walked up to where he was standing.

"Another month or so. I think the steel is what pushed our schedule back. But the boys will be done soon."

Tori walked around the site, there was noise coming from someone drilling in one of the units. Noise from the concrete mixer. Noise in another unit. Someone was welding the steel to make staircases. The units were looking good. A little smile creased the corner of Tori's lip as she looked at her dream take shape. It had been worth it; leaving secular work, claiming her inheritance, and convincing her parents that the money was going to good use. Her parents had actually only agreed to her claiming the money when Tori produced her plans. Finding the two plots had been easy. Tracking down the owners of the plots had been a nightmare. After a number of visits to Council and Land Board she eventually did find the owners. One had been a widow who had acquired the plot after her husband died a few years back. She had no plans to make improvements. Purchasing the plot in the first place had been her husband's idea not hers. She did not mind relinquishing ownership and pocketing the money from the sale. The other had been a businessman with grand plans. Unfortunately for him and fortunately for Tori, he had lost his job and was struggling to stay afloat, so he agreed to let the plot go.

Applying for the water and electricity had not been as much of a headache as Tori had anticipated. She paid the application fees and was given a date of inspection.

Stacy's men were doing final touch-ups by mid-October. The man had been true to his word. The work was immaculate. This chubby cheeked brawn had been decent, though when they first met she had been convinced that he had sloth-like habits.

"I am glad Poppy suggested you when I was asking around in Francistown."

"It has been a pleasure working with you Miss Amin. You are one of the few who have all their ducks in a row."

"What do you mean?"

"Most people cannot finish projects like these, this quickly. Money is always an issue."

Tori shook her head. Well, money would have been a problem for her too if her parents hadn't come through with the trust fund, she thought to herself. "Well, I am glad we worked well together."

"Now all you need to do is furnish the place. No more sleeping in your truck."

Tori's eyes popped.

"You didn't think we knew," he smirked.

Tori massaged her neck and shook her head sheepishly.

"You did well though. It kept us on our toes. Your enthusiasm was infectious."

"Well Stacy, thank you so much for doing a grand job."

"You are welcome. You can go in and have a look." Stacy smiled, as he removed a fag from its packet and lit it.

The smell caused Tori to back track. She pulled the cigarette from his wide lips, threw it to the ground, and stubbed it out, before darting Stacy a disapproving glare.

He chuckled and walked to pick up a few tools to load in his truck.

As Tori walked into the first unit, it was as though she was seeing the place for the first time.

The loft apartments had an industrial chicness to them. The hard steel staircase and beams gave the apartment a masculine feel. Yet the wooden surfaces and the large glass walls softened the textures bringing in needed light and gentleness to the lofts. The glazed concrete floors highlighted the simplicity of the lofts. Tori had selected the craft brick elements to match the individually picked furniture she had ordered two months back. The container was scheduled to arrive this week. Tori had only been able to afford furniture for one of the apartments. She reasoned that the furnished one would help furnish the rest. She was acutely aware that her pockets finally bore holes and she would be living on a shoestring for the next couple of months.

That week Tori moved from the unoccupied BHC house to Loft One, it was as though she was dreaming, a place of her own at last. The plan was to rent out two lofts to tourists and use the third as her own base.

That week, as she waited for the container with the furniture to arrive Tori connected the internet and set up an Instagram and Facebook page for her new business, but she could not think of what to put up. The lofts were all empty.

Tori's phone vibrated. It was Mpho.

"Hey."

"Hey hey, how are things coming along?"

"Can you believe they are done!"

"What, that was fast!"

"Yah, and I am out of capital. I don't know what I am going to do if all this goes south."

"Don't worry yourself about that. There is business in Kasane. Have you started advertising yet?"

"Not really actually, I was thinking of enquiring around on what the prices are like then use that to kinda come up with a rate so I don't cheat myself, or overcharge my customers."

"That's a good idea."

"I'm sorry I haven't been over. Things have been crazy with the little one."

"Yah, you mentioned she was unwell."

"Mmm, the fever wasn't going away, she was in bed for a good month, and the doctors don't even know what the problem was. She just had flu-like symptoms, but when given the usual flu meds the fever wouldn't subside."

"That's bizarre, I hope she regains her health quickly."

"Thanks."

"How are things with Mark? Every time I see a wild animal roaming around I can't help but think of the scene we saw with that herd of buffalo. Speaking of which, did he ever find out what killed those buffalo that time? I have been so busy with this project I have hardly been in touch."

"Mmm, no, I understand. Bella has kept me on my toes as well; I have also been rubbish at keeping in touch. That buffalo case, they still haven't figured out what the issue was. And it looks like the whole thing has died down. The samples they took that time were tampered with by an overzealous intern, and the case went cold, so nothing on that score."

"That's a shame. After all the work Mark and Glen did."

"I know neh," Mpho was silent for a second, before blurting, "Apparently Glen has been asking after you."

Tori rolled her eyes. "What was he asking?"

"No, just how you are doing."

"I hope you didn't encourage him."

"Tori, I thought you wanted to settle?"

"Mpho, I have no time to settle. I have just started a business; the last thing I want is to be tied down."

"Settling down is not the same as being tied down."

"I know. But I wouldn't give him the attention he would want."

"How would you know that?"

"Mpho, if you had seen me these past few months you would have seen that I do not have time for a man."

"I still can't believe you ran away from that Austrian guy when he asked you out."

"Why are you bringing up that old story?"

She could hear Mpho laughing on the other end of the receiver. "Tori, you are the one that is always saying you love what Mark and I have. What do you think; he and I were born chained at the hip? No, we met more or less the way you meet all these eligible bachelors and we hit it off. Was I scared? Yes, one hundred percent. I was terrified that he was going to rip my heart to shreds. But that is what love is about; you need to trust that person to some degree at the onset. And when you do let your guard down, sorry to say, you will get burnt now and then. But you, you are protecting your heart with a steel wall as though something seared it."

Tori was quiet.

"Well, I was willing to give Bas…"

"Don't say that name. You and I both know that man is bad news."

"How do you know the Austrian isn't bad news, and how do you know Glen isn't bad news."

"They both didn't give off reptilian vibes when I met them. That man has the word 'player' tattooed on his forehead. You were too blind to see them."

"Well. I have a ton of things to do before I go to bed."

"I know you are trying to avoid this conversation."

"No I am not," Tori sighed.

"What is it?"

"Fine, I will give them a chance?"

"Give who a chance?"

"Glen or Gabe, whichever G comes searching for me first."

"Great."

"Please don't go running to Mark telling him that Glen should make a move first, I would like it to happen naturally."

"Babe, I think we are way past natural. I let you do the natural thing a year ago, and you ran in the other direction. You need help, sugar. Lots of help."

Tori couldn't help but smile. "I need a glass of wine. I may be broke, but at least I can still afford a fifty pula bottle."

"Okay, I will let you go. Will chat with you soon. You should send me pictures after you place the furniture."

"Sure thing."

Tori was at the bottle store in town pacing down the red wine aisle looking for something smooth to soothe her bones. She crouched down to scrutinize one of the bottles on special. It was Tin Cups merlot/cabernet sauvignon. She pulled the bottle off the shelf before propelling herself to an upright posture, as she did, she noticed Gabe walk into the bottle store followed by a blonde lady. She was whispering something to him which caused Gabe to lean into to her. Tori quickly walked to the cashier, there were two other people in front of her. The couple was still browsing through the bottle store aisles. Tori flipped her thick hair to the right, so it could hide her face. One person was now in front of her. The cashier scanned the man's items. The machine stopped. The woman looked at it blankly. Meanwhile, Gabe and his babe had picked whatever they had come into the store to buy and were making their way to the till. Why was there only one till in this store? It didn't make sense. Tori's hands were sweating; her breathing was intensifying with each of Gabe's advancing steps. The woman at the till was changing the receipt roll. Tori was about to leave the bottle of wine and make a dash for the door when she heard her name. She plastered a smile on her face and squirmed as she turned.

"Gabe!" she put on a surprised voice.

"What are you doing here?"

"Oh," Tori's eyes darted from Gabe to the babe, then back at Gabe. "I…" she cleared her throat, "I live here."

"Never!"

Tori nodded, the fake smile still plastered on her face.

"Oh wow. That is so bizarre, we just moved here too."

"We?" she asked.

"Oh, yes. Becky and I moved to Kasane about a month ago."

"Hi." Tori gave an awkward single wave to the right.

"Next," the cashier called.

Like a revolving door, Tori tilted to face the cashier. She paid for her cheap wine and nodded to Gabe and his babe before escaping the scene, finding sanctuary in her car.

The next morning Tori was woken up by her phone ringing. She opened up one eye. Her head was pounding, when she finally pulled herself from the floor there was a sticky substance that clung to the left side of her face. A vulgar smell stung her nostrils. She scratched through the pile of clothes that had been flung across the room.

"He… hello."

"Ah, glad we got a hold of you. The container has arrived. Do you mind sending us directions or coming to meet us at Nandos? We are actually at the filling station next to Nandos."

"Oh, does your phone have GPS?"

"Yes ma'am."

"Okay, I think it would be best if I dropped you a pin."

"Very well madam. Thank you."

Tori tried to backtrack. How did she end up in a pile of vomit? Her memory took her back to the liquor store. "Gabe… Eish, the babe," she shuddered.

She moved as fast as she could to clean up the mess, ventilate the loft, take a shower and look presentable. The delivery truck arrived fifteen minutes after the call. The men were jovial. When they saw Tori, they jumped out of the vehicle and greeted her with a receipt.

"What is this?"

"Oh, customs ma'am."

"What do you mean, I paid for everything."

"Yes, and we paid for customs. You need to pay this amount."

Tori gapped when she saw the amount. She barely had a hundred pula in the account and the man was demanding close to fifteen thousand. She looked at the receipt again and shook her head. "But I paid for everything."

"Yes mama, you paid for all the furniture, for the shipping container, and for the shipping itself. But they failed to add the customs charge. Our freight covered that so you can have your items delivered to your doorstep as you had requested."

The man was Zulu, speaking with a lilting English, and a very open manner about him. Tori had picked it up the first time she had talked to him twenty minutes earlier over the phone. "Okay, give me a minute."

Tori's mind was swirling. She didn't know where she was going to conjure 15k from. "Not mother," she mumbled as she walked into her left. "Mpho." Tori picked up the phone. "Hey."

"Hi. What's up?"

"The furniture is here."

"Oh, great! Have you offloaded? Send me pictures."

"Can't really offload at the moment. I have a receipt in my hand, the man is asking for 15k."

"15k for what!" Mpho's shock was apparent.

"Customs."

"Heh banna!"

"Exactly! I am all out of money. And I don't want to call mom or dad, or even my brothers. Can you and Mark help out?"

Mpho was quiet for a few minutes. "Let me call you back."

Tori was glaring at the phone when the men walked in, "Should we start offloading?"

"Give me one second please," she started tapping on her phone screen. Her head was throbbing, causing her to feel green about the gills.

Ten minutes had passed. The men walked in again. "Mama," the man who had handed Tori the receipt was tapping at his wristwatch. "We are driving back to South Africa today, sisi."

"Yes, one moment." Right then her phone rang

"Hey?"

"Mark is asking which account we should send the money to."

Tori heaved a sigh of relief. "Let me take a picture of the receipt and the account details and send it to you via WhatsApp."

"Sure."

"Thank you soooo much!"

"What are friends for? You've come this far, this is just the last hurdle."

"Let me send you the details right now."

Tori quickly sent the details to Mpho, and gestured to the men to start offloading. The man with the Zulu accent approached Tori.

"The customs issue sisi?"

"We are wiring the money to the account as we speak."

"Okay, so let us wait for the boss to call, and then we will offload."

Fifteen minutes later and still there was no activity. Tori was about to call Mpho when she noticed the men starting to move. They opened the container and started to offload its contents.

"Where would you like us to put these things, mama?"

Tori perked up. Her headache receded, and she got to work with the men that were offloading. It was five in the evening by the time she had the things placed just the way she wanted them. The men had left right after offloading, leaving Tori to push, shift and pull things to her liking. All she needed now were a few ornaments, paintings, and plants to make the place look cozy. She was strapped for cash, so the décor and the garden would have to wait. She couldn't exactly ask Mpho for more money, nor go groveling to her siblings or parents. "I will just have to charge minimum rates until I have the place looking up to scratch." That evening Tori slept at midnight. She had spent the rest of the day taking pictures at every angle. On the Instagram and Facebook accounts she had signed up for earlier, she got to work beefing up the pages with the pictures she had taken so they would look appealing. She then boosted the pages to The United Kingdom, America, Australia, and Europe. With satisfaction, she scrolled through her pages checking for errors and tweaking a few things. She smiled at the name she had picked for her three lofts, Peter's Place.

Guests

IT WAS ON A HOT SUNDAY AFTERNOON in mid-November when Tori got an enquiry on her loft, a couple from Italy were looking to come for a vacation in Kasane.

Loft one has dressed with boho-chic interiors that embodied coziness. The contemporary comforts Tori had captured with the layout of the furniture drew one in. The loft was something rare in Kasane, something unique, something really special. What the exterior lacked, the interiors made up for it. The natural light let in by the wall-length glass windows bounced on the white walls and seemed to dance on every inch of the property. The prime location of the property also gave the lofts uninterrupted views of the Chobe. From the top balcony, which was the perfect lookout point, one could see as far as Namibia. It smelled like home, which was what Tori wanted. She wanted her guests to spend their days exploring what Kasane had to offer, and then come back to the loft and feel at home. Tori had deliberately not installed any TVs in the loft. She wanted her guests to focus on nature, which was part of the brief she had shared with the architect who designed all three lofts; to have unobstructed views filling the house into the outdoor space, so you are outside and inside. A tourist's dream!

She had priced her lofts at a bargain price of three thousand pula per night, being able to house four guests per night. She reasoned that she could up the price once the garden was done up and a pool had been installed. After a few back and forth correspondence with the couple, Tori bagged her first booking. The couple was set to arrive the following week on a Sunday and would spend an entire week at Peter's Place. They insisted on paying upfront. Before the day was over, Tori had twenty-one thousand in her account.

"Send me your account details," she smiled into the phone as she spoke to Mpho.

"What is it?"

"I just had my first booking!" Tori was so excited she started to scream.

Mpho on the other end started to scream too.

The friends laughed uncontrollably as they celebrated Tori's achievement.

"Can you believe I was on my last can of beans?"

Mpho was still laughing, "Have you been on a bean diet tsalu? Why didn't you tell me you needed more money, Mark and I would have sent you some?"

Tori shook her head, as though she was standing in front of Mpho. "No, I couldn't have done that to you guys. You both have been so generous. I didn't wanna push it."

"I get it, but still we would have lent you the money."

"I know."

"So? First guests. Where are they from?"

"Italy. They will be staying a week. So at least it covers the fifteen that I owe you, and I can use the rest of the money to buy a few things to decorate the loft. I wanna stay true to Bots, so I am thinking of going to that old lady's gift shop in a minute."

"She had some cool stuff."

"Yah, I just hope she will be open on a Sunday."

"Well, send me pictures once you have put up the décor."

After Tori deposited the money for Mark and Mpho, she saddled up in her Surf and made her way into town. The gift shop was open, to Tori's surprise. She walked in with a spring in her steps. The old lady was sitting behind the counter, beak in a book. When she heard the door chimes she popped her head up to see who it was.

"Hello, darling. How are you this Sunday? And why aren't you at church? Sunday is a day that you should be thinking about the lord."

Tori nodded as she walked around the shop wondering why the old lady had not gone to her church to pay homage to her lord, but she did not say that out loud. Instead, she smiled and asked if there were any African paintings in stock.

"Oh yes, I only keep local artists. There are some lovely paintings by a boy who used to live in Kasane, now he has moved, greener pastures and all. Here they are." She pulled a few paintings from under her counter and laid them on top for Tori to have a look at. All signed Roger Brown. His technique was captivating; Tori immediately fell in love with his artistry. She picked three paintings and promised to come for more.

"Wonderful," the woman smiled. "My Samantha says she has booked a stay at Peter's Place?"

Tori was taken aback.

"Yah, everyone knows you have been building those beautiful lofts that overlook the river. My niece has been planning to visit for some time now, but with things between me and Gerald going a bit sour, I didn't have a place to put her up with her Italian husband. They met in Kasane, you know, a few years back. At The Old House, just down the road."

Tori shook her head, "No, she never mentioned."

"Yes. And they have been meaning to come back. It's her fifth anniversary next week. So I recommended Peter's Place. You need the business I assume. Even though I have never seen the lofts, I figured you could do with some referrals."

Tori was thoughtful for a moment. "Would you like to come over for dinner tonight, so I can show you around? The lofts are not all finished yet. But loft one is done, and ready for your niece and husband." Tori felt it was the least she could do to thank this Good Samaritan for helping her bag her first customer.

"That sounds like a treat. I will drive over around six this evening if that is okay with you?"

"Sounds perfect. Is there anything you don't eat? Do you have any food allergies?"

"No, never have. I eat anything from mopane worms, to tswii," the old lady crowed.

Tori smiled as she made her way to the door. "Six o'clock."

The babushka pulled up at Peter's Place at five forty-five. Tori met her outside and ushered her in.

"Oh wow, this truly is a cozy little spot, isn't it? I know my Samantha and Gregory will be very comfortable here."

Tori smiled warmly at the aged woman before she walked to the kitchenette, picked up a glass of ice tea she had made in anticipation of her guest, and gingerly handed it to her.

"Venus."

"Sorry?"

"My name, it's Venus. You can call me Aunt Venus if you like," the wrinkles on her face intensified as she gave Tori a sincere smile.

"Well Aunt Venus, I hope you love shepherd's pie because that is what we are having tonight."

"I haven't had shepherd's pie in years," Venus said as she walked around the loft. "I have never seen a house like this before." She stopped at the paintings that Tori had purchased earlier at her shop. "These fit in really well here."

"I couldn't agree more," Tori smiled as she dished the pie onto two stoneware plates. "Would you like a refill?" She offered more ice tea.

"No, I am good. This is enough to fill my bladder. Anymore, and I will be having accidents in the middle of the night. That would really set off my Gerald," she chuckled.

Tori blinked rapidly, unsure if she should smile or just keep a straight face. The old woman was bent on sharing the life lived with her Gerald, which unnerved Tori a little. "So you say you are from Zim?"

"Oh, yes, Gweru to be exact. Our family was originally from England. My great-grandmother and father settled in Zimbabwe years ago. They farmed the land. Zimbabwe used to be the breadbasket of the world. Botswana used to buy its produce in Zimbabwe. It was a beautiful country, it still is. It's just that power and greed sometimes overshadow what is most important in life," she giggled, as she shoved a spoonful of pie into her mouth. "Did you know, Zimbabwe means home of stone, interesting little nugget. My mother still lives there. She is ninety-seven years old."

Tori shook her head in disbelief.

"Yes," the old woman chuckled. "She is made of strong bones, that one. I am sure she is going to outlive us all."

"And you moved to Botswana when?"

"We moved in December of nineteen sixty-four. I was ten years old. Gold rush and all. My dad thought Botswana was the place to be at the time. I do sometimes wish we could have lived longer in Zim.

"Oh wow!"

"Yes, but I was a child, children don't make big decisions do they," she chuckled.

"And you and Gerald met how?"

"I was in Francistown for a while before I met my Gerald.

Beautiful town. Do you know why Blue Jacket Street is called Blue Jacket Street?"

Tori shook her head.

Venus gurgled, "It's funny really. It was named after an old prospector Sam Anderson because he was always seen on the street wearing a denim blue jacket," she laughed. "Funny reason to give a street a name, but there you have it."

Tori forced a smile.

"And Francistown got its name from a man called Daniel Francis. He helped to organize and establish the town back in the day. The city has a lot of history. It was one of the sites of Southern Africa's first "gold-rush." That Tati River had gold in it. And the areas surrounding it. I wouldn't be shocked if there still is gold around that area that they missed when excavating back then."

"What did you and Gerald do?"

"We owned a farm. Not as big as the one the Sono's own, but something along those lines. My Gerald loves all things animals. He studied to be a zoologist in South Africa, has the certificates for it and all. He is Afrikaana you know? Grew up there and all. He moved to Francistown a few years before we started courting, for a job under the wildlife department, working in the lab until there was an incident," she snarled, "they accused my Gerald of tampering with something, and he lost his job. Can you imagine?" She raised her voice, "my Gerald, tampering with stuff, absolute nonsense!" Venus paused, shook her head, and rolled her eyes, "So we settled at the farm. He has the gift, and likes to tinker with things in his DIY lab," she added, her voice a lot calmer.

"Oh, shame," Tori said sympathetically. "You mentioned a farm, so you owned cattle?"

"Oh not just cattle, we had horses, sheep, goats, pigs, geese, pigeons. We could have opened up a zoo," Venus laughed.

"Wow, that is a lot!"

"It was. Eventually, we sold out, and decided to move up to Kasane."

"Why did you choose Kasane?"

"Why did you choose Kasane?" Venus smiled.

"I don't know." Tori walked over to the wine rack and poured two glasses of merlot. "I think it's the warthogs."

Venus shook her head. "It's more than the warthogs, dear. Kasane talks to you when you enter it. The town is like none other. It has an extremely vibrant community. Over the years, artists have travelled from abroad, seen the possibilities and opportunities, and decided to move here. We have painters, poets, elite photographers, who have left friends and family back in the western world and moved here. Have you noticed the lodge that is tucked away just around your bend?"

Tori shook her head.

"Ahhh, you still have a lot to see. There is an elite photographer's lodge just around the corner where renowned photographers come from around the world just to take pictures here in the Chobe."

"Really?"

"Yes, really. Kasane is a hidden gem. My Gerald and I call it one of the world's hidden wonders."

Tori loved the sound of that. "Well, I am glad I have made a home at one of the world's hidden wonders," she smiled.

"People don't try to dominate the animals that roam around. They don't try to push the animals away. They try their best to live along with them and not get in their way. Why do you think there are corridors left, right, and center around this town? The government has done a fantastic job in trying to preserve the natural state of this enchanting town. Have you noticed there is no fence that blocks the animals from roaming into town from the park?"

Tori shook her head, "It's amazing and scary at the same time. My lofts overlook a bush, and then your eyes hit the river. There is no other building in sight from the balconies." She walked up to the glass door and slid it open, and sure enough, it was a bush. Nothing but nature."

"Mmm, this is beautiful, dangerous, but beautiful. I would suggest that you place electric fences around your property. Maybe a wall at the front, and then an electric fence at the back, and possibly cone-shaped spikes to keep the elephants from getting too close."

Tori was thoughtful.

"Lions roam around at night, dearest. As well as elephants, buffalo, and other wild critters. You don't want to be liable for someone getting eaten on your property."

The thought made Tori cringe. "You are right."

"I know I am right. That is what most lodges have done. Most, not all. They try to make sure their guests feel as though they are at one with nature, but also safe from it if you know what I mean."

"I think I just might do what you are suggesting. I would have to wait though. I have only had this booking that you so happily helped me out with. I have been living out-of-pocket for the past couple of months now. This project has bled me dry."

"Don't worry too much, you have invested in the perfect town. This place is never short of tourists. You will do well. You may be living like a pauper now, but very soon, your pockets will be well lined," she giggled.

"Would you like to see the view from the bedroom upstairs?"

"Oh, wow, I can't remember the last time I was upstairs. I hope my wobbly legs will be able to carry me," Venus followed Tori to the top.

"This bedroom is an observation tower," she chuckled as she

took in the scene the loft presented because of its elevated vantage point.

Tori opened the glass doors; there was a pair of egg-shaped wicker swing chairs.

Venus chuckled as she sat. "This is a real treat. Thank you for inviting me."

Tori smiled. She had found a friend in Venus. She was not sure yet what kind of friend she would be, but at least she had company. It was a lovely change from all the men that had surrounded her for half a year working on the lofts. Now that the project was over, Tori was able to sit back and enjoy the fruits of her labour. Having someone else enjoy it with her while listening to their opinion brought her joy.

After Venus left, Tori quickly washed up before finally reclining on the Barrali queen sofa sleeper she had purchased specifically for extra guests downstairs. The gray fabric was plush and simple. The clean lines and fresh aesthetic finishing had won her over when she first started looking for furniture. She had also purchased the throw pillows that went with the sofa. The abstract designs were contemporary, blending well with the whole look and feel of the loft. She reached out to her computer to check her page on airbnb.com, there was something in her inbox. When she opened the message it was from a family from the UK, they wanted to book the loft for the beginning of December. They were requesting account details. Their stay was for two weeks.

Life in Kasane was going to be epic.

As Tori pulled out the queen mattress that was made out of quality memory foam, she couldn't help but smile, her dream was coming true. The only thing that was missing was someone to share it with.

By the beginning of December Tori had bookings every week till mid-April the next year. Her clients heard about Peter's Place mainly through referrals. After a little help from Aunt Venus with the Italian couple's patronage, they referred friends to Peter's Place, and the news spread like wildfire. It was shortly after Tori had furnished the second loft, put up a screen wall out front, an electric fence out back as well as the spiky cones to keep the elephants at bay as Aunt Venus had suggested that Tori realized that she needed help with house-keeping.

It was on a Friday afternoon that the idea popped into her head. Why she had not thought about it before was a mystery. She had just finished purchasing a few succulents from Spar when she decided to jump across the road to buy a few African ornaments from the lady she once called on to purchase African prints. When she approached the stall she noticed that the lady's stock was minimal. Tori scanned the little stall in search of its owner.

"Yes mama," Tori heard a voice say. The woman was sitting in the corner. Like a chameleon, she had taken the colour of the fabric that was hanging behind her and was completely camouflaged.

"Hi?" Tori felt blind for a second wondering where the stall owner was.

The woman stood up, "Yes madam," baby hanging to her shriveled breast like a koala.

"Oh, there you are!" Tori smiled reassuringly. "I am in need of help."

"Yes, fabric, I have some coming from Zambia tomorrow mama."

"Oh, no... nooo... I was thinking of something else."

"Oh?"

"Yes," Tori cleared her throat, second-guessing herself. She wondered if the lady would be willing to leave her own business to come and assist someone else's business. "I was thinking, I don't know if this is something you would be willing to do, but I am in need of a little help. I know you are a working mother," she pointed at the scrawny child that was latched onto its mother. "But I was hoping that maybe you would consider coming to work for me." As the words left Tori's lips she realized how ridiculous they sounded. The woman was obviously content with running her own business.

"Working for you?"

"Yes, I have a BnB that I am running up in Plateau and I am in need of someone to help with housekeeping. I have been doing it on my own for some time now, but I now need assistance." Tori noticed she was rambling. As though throwing details of her ordeal would convince the woman to abandon her stall and come work for her.

The lady was thoughtful for a second. She tucked in her wrinkled breast, and swung her offspring on her spine, before tying it with a tjitenge. "Leave my stall and work for you?"

"I know you have your own business. I couldn't think of anyone else. I am new in town, the only person I could think of was you."

"Mhm," the woman had the coloring of a Khoisan.

"It honestly doesn't have to be you. Maybe you know someone who knows someone. Please, here is my card," Tori rummaged in her small cross-body leather bag and produced a business card. "Please call me if you think of anyone that could assist me. I would really appreciate it."

The woman nodded, leaving Tori feeling rather silly. What made her think that her offer was far better than what the woman was doing? As she unlocked her car, she shook her head, "you are basically saying she should leave her stall to go and clean up after people, clean dirty toilets and showers!"

When she pulled in at her property she noticed that the garden boy had arrived.

"Hello madam," the short man smiled at Tori.

"Small boy, o teng?"

"Yes, ke teng. Did you manage to get more shrubs and plants?"

"Yes, they are in the back."

Small boy walked to the back of the Surf and started to offload. Tori walked into loft three which she had asked the architect to tweak slightly, so it did not look identical to the other two. It was her personal space, her home, her abode. She still did not have enough money to furnish it, but the loft had been designed to embody a more woodland theme. Instead of steel beams, Tori had insisted on wooden ones, and instead of steel stairs, she got wood. The layout at the top was designed to accommodate a bedroom for a bachelorette as well as a mini office. There was a lone round wicker chair with a metal base in the open living area. She placed her bag on the chair and walked to the fridge. There was a bowl of leftovers, pasta salad with blue cheese and bacon. She grabbed a fork, not bothering to dish it into a separate plate, and started eating.

A wine rack stood in solitude on the counter housing a bottle of Malbec she had picked up at Woolies. She reached for a glass and gently poured a generous amount. Her phone vibrated. She shoved more pasta in her mouth and washed it down with a sip of wine. She ignored her phone and walked out back. The wall that demarked her loft from the other two gave her the privacy she craved. A pergola with custom-fabricated, fixed-roman-solar shading panels had been installed a month back. These gave filtered shade. Tori smiled knowing that if she pulled her lone chair under the pergola there would be no prying eyes from the other two lofts gawking in her direction, the perfect little nook. She walked back into the kitchen and placed the bowl of salad on the island, before carrying the wicker to the backyard. Her phone vibrated again and then started ringing. She pulled open her bag. It was a number she didn't know.

"Hello?" Quizzical brow.

Pause.

"Who is this?" frown on forehead.

Pause.

"Oh, okay, I'll call you back now, now." Tori hung up the phone and called the number back. "Hello?"

Pause.

"Oh, did you find someone for me?" Small smile.

Pause.

"They can start as soon as possible." Smile widens.

Pause.

"I will discuss that with the lady when she comes in." Determined look.

Pause.

"Thank you so much, I look forward to meeting the lady tomorrow." Satisfied.

Tori sat watching the foliage that stretched on till it reached the Chobe. The view from the top was more enjoyable than from below. But she was too lazy to balance the chair in one hand and her glass of wine in the other and walk upstairs. She didn't mind though, the phone had her mind racing. She needed to sort out work arrangements with the new help. The person would need training. And they would need to be trustworthy. She wasn't looking to hire someone with sticky fingers. The last thing she wanted was bad reviews from guests because their diamond necklace went missing, or their iPad grew legs and walked out of Peter's Place.

Evening was setting, Tori could hear her neighbors having a whale of a time. Suddenly there was a knock on her door. Tori sat still for a few minutes hoping that the person would go away. She had earned herself the evening off after all. The knocking persisted.

"And this is why I need help," she huffed, before walking to the front door. "Yes?" she smiled.

"Sorry ma'am," a peppy, blond girl who resembled Elle Woods from Legally Blond beamed, "we were hoping to get a few more towels, we went swimming at one of the hotels downtown, and carried our towels with us, and now we are out of towels." She had this annoying nasal accent and her tongue seemed to get in the way of each word she uttered.

"Oh, sure," Tori walked up the stairs, picked up some fresh linen from one of her shelves, and walked back down. "Here you go."

"Thank you," the girl started to leave, "you know," she backed up. "It would be so cool to have a pool here at the lofts. It would save us the drive down to town. We just love it here," she smiled cheekily.

"I will consider your suggestion ma'am," Tori smiled.

The truth was Tori had been looking into installing a pool. She would have installed it when she first built the lofts, but money was tight. She had done a bit of research on pools; it was a toss-up between fiberglass or concrete. The fiberglass was easy maintenance, but expensive to install, and the concrete was cheaper to install, but the maintenance could be a bit of a problem. Now that the sorority girl had mentioned a pool, Tori was thinking more and more about it. She knew she could not afford to furnish her loft and at the same time build a pool. And while the pool was getting installed she knew business would stop for approximately six to fourteen weeks.

The Water Hole

MPHO AND MARK HAD arrived late last night.

The trio were in Tori's car on a quest to find the Water Hole. Apparently, it was a lodge that was nestled in the bush that elephants frequented.

"Do you trust your newfound aunt?" Mpho questioned.

"Well, it's an adventure either way. Whether it was gas talk or not, I won't worry about it now. I am enjoying the excursion with you guys."

"I wish we could have spent the day at the lofts," Mpho sighed.

"Yah, but the pool guys are just doing the last bits to complete the project. It would have been easier if I had installed the pool during the time the lofts were being constructed, but madi guys? Madi."

"Yah neh, the project was well worth it though," Mark remarked. "The architect did a brilliant job."

"Yah, my brother recommended the guy. I am glad I trusted his judgment," Tori said as she swerved sharply.

"I must admit, going back to him to design the pool as well, was a smart move," Mpho yawned.

"Mmm, I would have never thought to build one long rectangular pool that is demarcated pool for each of the first two lofts by miniature walls for privacy. It was a lot cheaper than building two separate pools. My pool is separate from the two. No fraternsing, Tori said with a mischievous smile plastered on her coco coloured face.

"When are you planning to reopen?" Mark asked.

"Well, truthfully, I haven't said the place is closed. So people abroad think it is just fully booked," Tori snickered, "that way I keep the anticipation high."

"Smart. When you see your favourite restaurant or store being renovated and there is nowhere else to find it, it is disheartening, so you were clever about it, and often than not, people find a different restaurant. That's how you lose customers." Mpho said, as she gazed out of the window.

"Mmm, this way I get to keep those customers. The competition here can be brutal at times."

The Surf came to a halt. Tori, Mpho and Mark had arrived. It was a uniquely handcrafted lodge. They made their way to the observation lounge. A waiter followed them shortly. He took their drink orders and left the light meal menu.

"Well looks like your aunt Venus was right. This place is pretty. I think I like how secluded it is." Mpho said walking to the edge of the deck. Gum poles had been used for elevation. If an elephant got too close you would be protected by the electric fence that was a meter away from the deck.

"Just be careful dear. They have mighty long trunks," Mark cautioned from the comfort of his chair.

Mpho smiled in response as she took a couple of selfies with the ellies in her background.

"So how have you been?" Mark turned his attention to Tori.

Tori exhaled, "It has been brutal, I must say. I never thought a project like this would take so much out of me, but it did."

"Mmm?"

"Yah. For one, I was living out of my car."

"What? On-site? With all those men? Tori!" Mark tilted his head disapprovingly.

"No, no," Tori stretched out her hand to give Mark a reassuring pat. "I parked my car at an empty BHC house around the corner. "

"Where did you bathe, or cook, or use the bathroom?" Mark still had a disapproving look, this time coupled with a frown.

"I rotated around the lodges, my guise; swimming," Tori smiled proudly.

Mark shook his head, "It saved you a lot of money I guess."

"It sure did. Money I really needed. I had to furnish the lofts one by one, I couldn't afford to have them furnished at the same time. I am still working on mine. I shouldn't say mine really."

"Why?"

"I am thinking of letting out all three lofts."

"But why, I thought you wanted to always be near?"

"I do, but not that close. I get guests knocking at my door at odd hours of the day."

"Mhm."

"Mmm, there is a plot I have identified. It is not far from the lofts. I am thinking of making it the office as well as my home. That way when I have locked up the office, there is no way the guests can access my premises. The architect is still working on the plan."

"Kare, you don't waste time."

Tori shrugged. "The lofts have really been able to generate a good amount that by the end of the year, if not next year, I should be able to start building."

"Nice. And what about settling down? Have you had any thoughts yet?"

"Erm," Tori felt a little uncomfortable discussing her love life with her best friend's husband. "I haven't really thought about dating yet?"

"Why not?"

"I guess maybe it's 'cause I have been so busy."

"Dating doesn't stop you from carrying on with your projects."

"It's a distraction."

"How so?"

"You know, you become obsessed with the person, and your time gets diverted to that individual."

"Is that so? And you are talking from experience?" Mark chortles, as he takes a sip from his glass.

Mpho watches the pair from where she was standing, she couldn't be bothered to join them, the elephants were of more interest to her. She took a sip from her wine glass and took a few more selfies.

Tori giggled, "Why are you teasing me?"

"I am not. I am just shocked at your repulsion to the idea of dating!"

"I am not repulsed."

"So what is it? Glen likes you, you know."

Tori rolled her eyes, "Not you too."

"What?"

"Mpho has been on my case as well."

"So, what is the problem? He has a fat nose?"

"He does?" Tori asked, one brow raised in shock.

"No," Mark chuckled, "I am trying to figure out what features are turning you off."

"Oh," Tori smiled. "He is good-looking. I think in my mind, I just haven't been able to move away from thinking of dating anyone that is not," Tori gestured at herself.

"You are half Motswana aren't you?"

"Yes I know, but my father would have a fit if I married someone that is not," Tori circled her hand in the air in front of her face.

"Of Asian descent?" Mark assisted.

"Exactly."

"How come you have never mentioned this before? Gape it doesn't make sense, your father is married to a black woman!" Mark was perplexed.

"I know. It doesn't make sense to me either. I have a feeling that deep down inside he doesn't really care who I get married to. I know he and mom had a hard time when they wanted to get married. Both families were opposed. So I have a feeling he doesn't want me to go through the same thing," Tori paused, then exhaled heavily. "Dating has always been an issue for me. Even when growing up. I think it's because I am not attracted to men of, as you say Asian descent. There are attractive men that are Asian, don't get me wrong. It's just that I am more attracted to…"

"Caucasian men?"

"Yes," Tori admitted shyly, "and black men."

Mark raised a brow.

"What?" Tori hid behind her glass of wine.

"I just didn't think you were attracted to men like us."

"Oh, I am. In fact, there was a guy that I went to school with, Sebastian. I have always had a crush on him, but never acted on it."

"Why not?"

Tori shrugged her shoulders.

Mpho approached the pair, "I hope you are not telling my husband about that player that had you under a spell the last time we were here," Mpho interrupted.

"I didn't realize you were eavesdropping," Tori said rolling her eyes.

"Love, that man is bad news," Mpho said as she walked over and took a seat next to her husband.

"Why do you say that," Mark was intrigued.

"For one, he kept licking his lips."

Tori's face flushed, she guffawed loudly as she tried to mask her embarrassment as Mark's eyes pierced through Tori.

"Guys, stop…" Tori stood up and walked to the edge of the deck. "Why do I feel like I am being interrogated here?"

Mpho and Mark sat quietly as they stared at Tori.

"I know I want to be with someone eventually," Tori said, turning her back to the ellies.

Mpho made a face.

"Stop Mpho. I know what you are thinking, and yes, I am afraid. I am afraid of getting hurt. I am afraid of falling for the wrong guy. I am afraid of not being compatible with someone after investing time and emotions. I am afraid of falling in love with someone I know my parents would disapprove of. I am afraid that the guy will not be able to handle my parents if I do eventually pluck up the courage to choose Glen or Gabe." Tori flung her hand in the air. "Agh, what am I talking about anyway, Gabe is with someone else."

"Since when?" Mpho said as she stood up and walked towards Tori.

"Who is Gabe," Mark was lost.

"Oh, that's that pilot. He asked Tori out and she ran away from him like a scalded canary."

"It's a scalded cat, not a canary," Tori rolled her eyes at Mpho.

"You know what I mean. The point is, you were scared."

"Why would Gabe asking you out scare you?" Mark also stood

and walked to where the ladies were standing, his gaze fixed on Tori.

I don't know," Tori lied.

"It's because she likes him," Mpho interjected.

Mark's brow jerked up.

Tori took a sip from her glass. Silence ensued.

Kgaphamadi

I T WASN'T NAMED AFTER a famous historian. Nor was it named after a politician. Neither was it named after a traveler back in the day that discovered something, named it something else, and documented it, even though that same thing had already been discovered by its local inhabitants. No, Kgaphamadi was named after the notorious shenanigans that went on in that location. In Gaborone, you had Old Naledi. In Selebi Phikwe you had Botshabelo, and in Francistown, you had Maipaafela, and in actual fact, you had a Kgaphamadi as well. All these locations had more than one thing in common, mismatched poorly built homes, barefooted dirt-covered children happily playing in the streets with their custom made wire cars, random mechanic shops, outside kitchens, pit latrines, dirt roads, a sgothi, a semausu at every corner, a crazy man roaming the streets and of course, pregnant teens.

Lesedi was one such pregnant teen. She had fallen in love at the age of thirteen when she had first been admitted at Chobe Junior. By the second term, the poor girl was pregnant. It was wintertime, so she was able to hide her bloated stomach for a few months. When the third term came, she had fallen off the register. She named her first child Ketshepileone. Her second which she bore the following year was called Keeme, two years passed; Lesedi bore yet another child, Kepaletswe.

The family was of no consequence to the community, they neither made a difference nor planned on making a difference. Their mission seemed to be increasing the numbers for the population census. Lesedi was the fourth offspring of six, to a mother who fed the family from selling magwinya le mafresh (fat cakes and fresh chips) to the students at Chobe Junior. The first two were men, who worked at the safari companies in Kasane and had families of their own, adding to the clan. The third, a lady, worked at one of the lodges, she and her three offspring lived with the family in the two and a half house in Kgaphamadi. Lesedi had increased the mouths to feed. Had no job, so she couldn't contribute toward feeding the team of infants that was being manufactured at this address. Her younger siblings, twin girls were both still in standard five.

It was when Lesedi had given birth to Kepaletswe that her mother urged Lesedi to find work. "Each must feed their own. If you are old enough to bear children, you are old enough to feed them. This is not a nursery home, I never asked for extra kids to be feeding. Feed your children."

That was what prompted Lesedi to start looking for work. With no academic qualifications a result of not having completed her education, it was difficult to find a well-paying job; one that could help feed her offspring. It was by happenstance that she stumbled across a lady from Zambia who was selling African print. She gave Lesedi the idea to purchase fabric from her and sell to tourists after adding a bit of mark-up. After borrowing some money from her sister, Lesedi proceeded to apply for a slot at council so she could man her own stall. The next step after registering was to erect a stall. She got to work putting four corner posts using mopane trees, for her roof, she used abandoned industrial plastic. Pallets served as shelving for the accessories, ornaments, and pottery she had purchased from another lady from Kenya. To display her African print, she hung samples of the fabrics around the stall. Business was slow and most of the tourists preferred other stalls to hers. The ladies in neighboring stalls had better displays, and their stalls had been professionally erected. Making them look more welcoming.

On one hot unsuccessful sales day, two women walked by. One

looked like a mix of some sort. She wasn't pure Motswana, she had rich curly hair, hazelnut skin, and an aquiline nose. Yet she spoke pure Setswana with her friend. The women walked into Lesedi's stall, admired a few things, asked for prices, and ended up paying a hundred pula for a unique pair of earrings. At first, she had placed them back, but Lesedi figured the lady must have pitied her, after seeing the gap in her teeth, which had resulted from a fight she had gotten into with Keeme's father. He had defaulted on child support, and Lesedi had reported him, the result, a gap in between her decaying bites. Lesedi didn't care, if the gap was going to get her more customers, she was willing to smile all day. Kepaletswe was also a strategic move. Pity was what she was working with, and pity is what she got. Kepaletswe, unbeknown to her, was playing a key role in assisting her mother. Her clinginess and snotty routine was causing some customers to throw money at Lesedi. The routine lasted a few months, and then business started to die down again. Lesedi started to think that maybe pity wasn't a good hat trick after all.

"Tourists want to enjoy themselves when they are on vacation. You can't keep pulling the 'woe is me routine' on them. They have their own poor in their own countries. You need a new approach mami." Lesedi's sister spat at her after she divulged how business was going. "I want my money. You said you would pay me back after two months. It's been what, three? Pay me back, or sell your stock."

Close to a year passed, Lesedi was able to scrape by and pay her sister half of what she owed. She was failing to make enough to also contribute food at home. Her mother had threatened to throw her and her children out if she was not able to come up with money for rent and food by the end of the month.

It was on a Friday afternoon that a spark of hope fell on Lesedi's lap like a little tuft of cotton. The hazelnut woman was back. Her hair neatly tied in a bun. She had on a crisp white button-down shirt that looked one size too big, with distressed skinny jeans. Her shoes were flat and pointed, also white. Lesedi watched as the lady scanned the room.

"Yes mama," Lesedi had asked.

"Hi," the woman blinked, as though adjusting her eyes.

Lesedi noticed that the woman was still searching for her so she stood up. "Yes madam," Kepaletswe hanging on the breast of her mother as always. "Oh, there you are," the woman smiled. "I am in need of help."

"Yes, fabric, I have some coming from Zambia tomorrow mama," Lesedi lied. She wasn't sure why she lied, perhaps in a last-ditch effort to keep a customer interested in her stall. She knew her business was sinking, she did not know what else to do. Soon she would be on the streets with her kids. Her mother threatened Lesedi with eviction each day.

"Oh, no... nooo... I was thinking of something else."

"Oh?"

"Yes," the woman cleared her throat, she stood awkwardly just on the edge of the stall. "I was thinking, I don't know if this is something you would be willing to do, but I am in need of a little help. I know you are a working mother," the lady pointed at Kepaletswe. "But I was hoping that maybe you would consider coming to work for me." The woman seemed unsure of herself as she uttered her proposal.

"Working for you?"

"Yes, I have a BnB that I am running up in Plateau and I am in need of someone to help with housekeeping. I have been doing it on my own for some time now, but I am finding with the second loft up and running I am in need of assistance." The woman seemed to ramble on.

Lesedi couldn't believe what she was hearing. This woman was her savior. This could just be what she needed. Lesedi tucked in her shriveled breast, and swung her Kepaletswe onto her back, using a cloth the locals called a tjitenge to secure her. "Leave my stall and work for you?" Lesedi was still in disbelief.

"I know you have your own business. I couldn't think of anyone else. I am new in town, the only person I could think about was you."

"Mhm," Lesedi was thoughtful. She wondered when she could start the job.

"It honestly doesn't have to be you. Maybe you know someone who knows someone. Please, here is my card," the lady rummaged in her small leather bag and produced a business card. "Please call me if you think of anyone that could assist me. I would really appreciate it."

Lesedi nodded. She didn't have airtime. She couldn't afford to have airtime. She was thoughtful. "I could use mom's phone, then delete the phone log," she mused. A little spark of hope had been ignited in her. She would not be thrown away like an unwanted used shirt. She would be able to contribute. And maybe in the future as things progressed she would be able to find a place of her own. The thought made Lesedi giggle.

That afternoon, Lesedi knocked off early from work, she found her mother sitting on the unpolished stoop. Ketshepileone, Keeme, and their cousins were out on the streets playing with the neighbours' kids.

"Le tlhotse?"

"Mmmm."

"What is it?"

"I don't have enough for rent. I am afraid we might all get evicted."

"Ao?"

"Mmmm," Lesedi's mom sighed. "How was work?"

"No sales."

Lesedi saw the disappointment mask over her mother like a dark shadow.

"But I was offered a job."

"By the time you get paid at that job, we will be on the streets."

"Don't they need to at least give us a warning?"

"We have had warnings Lesedi," her mother's voice was strained.

Lesedi caught receipts and letters next to her mother by the corner of her eye. "Can I use your phone?"

"O batla go leletsa mang?"

"The lady that offered me the job."

With her boney right hand, the woman handed Lesedi her itel i2190 mobile phone locally known as a sedilame before taking a seat on the concrete floor. Lesedi un-tied the tjitenge that was holding her daughter from tumbling to the ground, before gently sliding Kepaletswe from her back to her thighs. She crouched down and sat next to her strikingly underweight mother. She pulled the business card she had been handed that afternoon and dialed the number then hung up. Waited a few minutes and tried again. Lesedi was hoping that the lady would ring her back. When that failed she decided to just call.

Hello? Lesedi could hear the question mark in Tori's voice.

"Hello?" Lesedi put on a cheery voice.

"Who is this?" Tori's voice was heard through Lesedi's mother's sedilame.

"It's Lesedi, the lady you gave your business card to at the stall. Do you mind please calling me back? I don't have enough airtime."

"Oh, okay, I'll call you back right now."

The phone went dead, and in a few seconds started vibrating.

"Hello?"

"Oh, did you find someone for me?" Tori's tone had changed to a more pleasant one.

"Yes, I did find someone, when can they start?" Lesedi held her breath.

"They can start as soon as possible," Tori responded.

"Oh wonderful, they will be ready to start tomorrow if that is okay? How much is the pay? Lesedi enquired.

"I will discuss that with the lady when she comes in."

"Okay, no problem. So tomorrow at Peter's Place?" Lesedi asked.

"Yes, that should be fine."

"Thank you, ma'am."

"Thank you so much, I look forward to meeting the lady tomorrow," and the line went dead.

Dusk Till Dawn

THE TRIO HAD BOOKED A SAFARI with Dusk till Dawn. The safari car was set to leave from a designated lodge. The game drive was scheduled for six in the morning. It was still a bit nippy so after introducing himself, the guide offered his guests ditonkana (vastly used affordable blankets with distinct patterns) to keep themselves warm. "We will be driving to the park in a few minutes. I just need to pack your breakfast," he smiled. The man had a deep bass that made Tori think of Mufasa from The Lion King. He hopped off the front and went to the rear of the jeep. Less than three minutes later he was strapped into the driver's seat with his foot on the gas. "There are no fences between the park and the town, which is why you see a lot of animals roaming around in town. We need to drive to the entrance of the park, and register before we can carry on," he announced.

Mark, Mpho, and Tori sat quietly in their seats enjoying the slow drive to the park's entrance. Once the vehicle was idle, the guide hopped out of the vehicle with a document in hand. He walked briskly into the little office by the park gate before hopping back into the vehicle, placed the jeep in first gear, and charged through the dirt road in the park.

The sun was making its debut for the day, its sharp rays piercing through the branches and shrubs. There was an earthy smell as the dirt was raised from the vehicle's tires. "Impala," Shadrack said, as he pointed at the skittish antelope. "They are called the McDonald's of the bush around here as they are fast food to predators," the man chuckled.

The warmth of the sun's rays permeated the woodland, giving the land the warmth it needed as well as warming up the three tourists that were huddled up in their seats.

"Phumba," the vehicle came to a standstill. "The warthog. It is an animal that is related to the common pig. They have flat heads, which have warts. The males have four warts, whereas the females have two. If you notice the tusks, they rub against each other, thus sharpening each other in readiness for battle."

"What do they eat?" Mpho enquired.

"They are herbivores, so they graze on grass. They also eat bulbs and roots. They use their snouts to dig. And, as you see, they go on their knees when grazing."

"Hang on," Tori butted in, "You said that they sharpen their tusks?"

"Yes?"

"With their warts?" Tori was perplexed.

"Not their warts. With their tusks."

Tori fell silent.

Shadrack turned the ignition key, bringing the vehicle to life. He went through a bend and increased the speed. "I am trying to get to the waterhole, to try and catch as many animals as possible. I hope you don't mind."

"No, not at all," Mark decided for the whole group. "Do what you need to do."

"Is this your first time here in Chobe?" the guide inquired.

"No, we have all been here before," Mpho said. "We were here just over a year ago. Remember when there was a case about the buffaloes."

"Oh, yes. That was a bizarre incident. And nothing has ever happened ever since. We in the wildlife community were worried.

If something like that were to take over the Chobe, can you imagine how much damage that would be?"

"Mmm, it's pretty frightening. It would change wildlife in Botswana as we know it." Mark shuddered.

"You see these trees," Shadrack pointed.

"You mean the dead trees?" Mpho asked.

"Yes, what do you think happened to them?" he quizzed.

"Water?" Mark volunteered.

"Yes, it could have been water."

"A disease, maybe?" Mpho asked.

"Yes, that too."

And you ma'am, what do you think could have killed them?" He posed the question to Tori.

"Elephants maybe? I know they are notorious for bringing down trees."

"All your answers are good, but none of you is correct. It was the Tsetse Flies. Between 1916 and 1955, there was a large outbreak of Tsetse Fly in Ngamiland which then spread to the Chobe region. The fly is well known for causing sleeping sickness. The fly has a very painful bite and can affect both flora and fauna. Once you are bitten you are lulled to sleep."

"Sleep?" Tori asked.

"Yes, death, you can die."

"Oh, wow, when you said sleep, I just thought you meant regular sleep."

"Oh, no. It's a lethal little fly. It causes a lot of damage," Shadrack stated.

"You say Tsetse Fly?" Mark queried.

"Yes, the guide said adamantly.

"That's an interesting theory, I work in the wildlife department and I have never heard of Tsetse Fly affecting trees in that manner. Water would do that, but not flies," Mark said firmly.

"The outbreak was so severe that the wildlife department actually came to the park and sprayed the area with a chemical called DDT."

"Oh," Mark recalled.

"Yes," Shadrack smiled. "So it is that chemical that affected these trees.

"That makes total sense. In my head, I was imagining Tsetse fly biting these trees and lulling them to sleep," Mark chuckled.

Shadrack burst into laughter too. "No. It's the chemicals that were used to kill the Tsetse fly that did the damage."

They were now on a long strip driving parallel to the Chobe.

"The Chobe River has its origins in the highlands of Angola where it is known as the Kwando. Eventually, the water pours into Linyanti, then it finally becomes Chobe. Once it crosses the border into Zambia, it meets the mighty Zambezi, which then tumbles into the gorges of the falls."

"Wow. It's one big river that keeps changing its name based on which country it is in," Mpho remarked.

"Mmm, and also depending on which part of the country you are in. Linyanti is still the same river as Chobe," Mark added.

"Yes, Chobe and Linyanti are very close together. There is a camp not far from here called Linyanti. It's just on the border of Chobe National park." Shadrack chopped in. His knowledge was impressive; every time he whipped up a fact the trio gave each other wide-eyed glances.

Hippos could be heard laughing in the water. The jeep slowed down its pace.

"Lions," Shadrack pointed.

Tori counted four; they were all lapping at the water. The landscape was a breathtaking kaleidoscope of gold and brown hues.

"Six," Shadrack announced, correcting Tori's thoughts.

On closer inspection, Tori noticed two cubs, the dominant male had been crouching, obstructing Tori's view. They sat in silence as they took in nature's wonders. A few antelope, giraffe, and zebra were standing behind a few bushes at a safe distance. Their heels ready to spring and dart for safety in anticipation of an attack. Mpho snapped a few pictures, exhaled, and let out a contented sigh.

"It's beautiful, isn't it?" Tori whispered.

"Absolutely glorious! I see why you have decided to move here," Mpho whispered back.

Suddenly the lions were startled. There was another jeep approaching. Shadrack turned on the ignition and moved on. "Let us give them a chance to enjoy the scene." He bobbed his head at the other guide and idled for a minute to chat with his comrade.

The man in the other jeep nodded at Tori, Mark, and Mpho, before stepping on the gas.

Shadrack carried on with the tour. A few elephants were around, herds of impala were scattered about. An odd bird was spotted here and there, however, Shadrack had something else in mind. He veered through the bush in search of a kill site. Eight minutes later and vultures could be spotted on treetops gawking at a carcass down below. The carcass emitted a strong stench. Lions were at the scene, and a pack of hyenas could also be spotted at a distance. The king of the beasts was the only one by the dead giraffe, with a few lionesses hovering around him as he tore at the dead animal's flesh. There were other vehicles around. The tourists were on the edge of their seats, each with a camera fit for high-profile Hollywood paparazzi. Shadrack found a spot in the frenzy before turning off the ignition. The scene was magnificent. Tori had never seen lions gathered for a meal.

"Normally the dominant male will eat first, as you can see before the rest of the family have their share. The females are the ones that usually do the work."

"You mean, they do the hunting," Mark stated.

"Exactly! At times, if it is a big animal, the male lions will also join in," Shadrack continued.

"They are sooo big, look at their paws," Mpho said between shots.

"Mmm, you don't want to find yourself in their grip," Mark added.

"There is no fence between the town and the park. Don't you ever have incidents?" Tori enquired.

"We do," Shadrack answered. "At times they roam the streets at night. But it is not very often. Lions do not like human interaction so they stay away," he added.

"And they can't see us right now?" Mpho questioned as the dominant male walked past their vehicle. He sauntered his way to a group of juveniles, walked past them then walked back to the group of females and cubs.

"Establishing his dominance," Shadrack captioned the act. "They can only see one object. If you make sudden movements that is when they will spot you, but if you stay still, all they see is one object."

"Wow!" Mpho gasped, as she snuggled closer to her husband.

"Over there you have four types of vultures, the Lappet-Faced, the White-Headed, White-Backed, and the Hooded vulture. The Hooded Vulture is the one that is always the first to arrive at a kill.

"Wow, that one looks very pale," Tori remarked.

"Mmm, that is a White-Headed vulture. The White-Backed is the most useless when it comes to hints to find a kill," Shadrack said as he consulted his watch. "It is almost time for us to head back. But we will stop at a nice spot for you to have something to eat." He revived the vehicle and turned his back on the scene.

The trees were bare, hardly any green on them. Shadrack now focused on the birds he spotted and gave a little caption on each. They saw Bateleur, Burchell's, Cape Spurfowl, Swainson's Spurfowl, the Saddle-billed Stork as well as the Marabou stork.

"The Hamerkop is a funny-looking bird and likes things," Shadrack smiled and chuckled as he reached a large baobab tree. He carefully looked around, before stopping the vehicle. He pointed at a large nest that had been constructed on the main fork of a large acacia tree. "It builds mansions," he smiled. "See its nest over there. The bird has a head of a hammer that is why it is called a Hamerkop. Kop is head in Afrikaans," he disembarked and announced a tea break before walking to the rear end of the jeep to offload the basket of food. He used the back end to serve. "You can use the toilet if you like,"

"Where?" Mpho asked.

"Go behind the tree or something," Tori said.

"But won't I get attacked by a lion, or a leopard or something?"

Shadrack walked around the enormous upside-down tree. "You are safe, we are actually at one of the designated stretch points," he announced before heading back to serve coffee to his passengers.

"Love, do you mind coming with me?" Mpho said to Mark. Her voice not convinced she would make it back to the jeep in one piece.

Tori walked towards Shadrack. Her eyes were peeled. Her fear was snakes. Her fear was that one day she would walk into her house and find a python curled up on the floor, or hanging from one of the beams.

"How would you like your coffee?"

"One teaspoon of sugar and some milk, please."

Shadrack obeyed. He smiled as he handed the enamel cup to Tori. "So you live here now?"

"Yes ma'am."

"I love Kasane, I own Peter's Place by Plateau."

"Oh, yes. I have seen the place. Your lofts look really nice."

"Thank you."

"And how is business so far?" Shadrack said, stretching the small talk.

"Not too bad. I just finished installing a pool. So it will pick up again."

"Yes, you made the right move. Here in Kasane you either start a little café, or accommodation, or safaris."

"And you, for how long have you done this?"

"I have been at it for three years now."

"Wow, you are from here?"

"Yes, I am from a little village out of Kasane called Kachikau. But I live in Kgaphamadi with my wife and kids."

Tori nodded as she took a sip of her coffee and bit into a muffin. Mpho and Mark reappeared from behind the bush. Shadrack warmly offered them both a hot beverage.

"You were saying something about that Hamerkop," Mpho prodded.

"Yes. It makes large nests, up to a meter and a half. The nests have many compartments in there. It's a funny bird actually; it uses sticks, and an assortment of human debris like glass, plastic, combs, even bicycle tire tubes." He sniggered.

"Wow, that is interesting!" Tori mumbled as she chewed the

chocolate chip muffins that were laid out.

After the trio was done with their snacks, Shadrack packed and saddled up. Mark, Tori, and Mpho embarked onto the Dusk till Dawn tattooed vehicle feeling quite refreshed.

"This tree you see here, the Baobab," he started as he reversed, "years ago it was used as a prison here in Kasane. If you go to the police station, which is a short walk from Chobe Safari Lodge, there is an ancient Baobab that was used as a prison. Up to fourteen people could be thrown in there."

Tori chuckled. "What do you mean thrown into the tree?"

Shadrack smiled. "Baobabs are hollow inside. You can see the size of this Baobab, the one next to the police station is bigger."

"Wow, you learn something new every day!" Mpho said, eyes wide, lips dropping in surprise.

The drive back was uneventful. A few birds were spotted and a few elephants were scattered about. Shadrack took a few sharp bends and passed a couple of dried-up ponds as he charged towards the park gate. Tori smiled contentedly as she took in the views, a new normal she would enjoy all her days in Kasane. She turned to gaze at yet another dried-out pond when she noticed in the distance a number of vultures descending at a rapid pace.

"Stop!" Tori shouted.

"Erm, we are running late ma'am," Shadrack said. "What did you see?" he asked reducing his speed reluctantly.

"Back up a bit please," she said, pulling up her binoculars.

Shadrack put the car in reverse.

"There," Tori pointed. "I see a large number of vultures descending there," she pointed. "Look," she handed the binoculars to the guide.

"You are right," the guide quickly gazed at his watch. He hesitated.

"It's okay, I am from the wildlife department, so you can blame me if you get into trouble," Mark said.

Shadrack was still not convinced. "The Chobe has specific routes, I can't go off route."

Mark nodded. "Well, let's follow the marked routes and if we do not reach the carcass then we can go on foot,"

"On foot! There are predators." Mpho interjected.

"Okay, let us go on the marked routes. If the carcass is off route, then I will notify the wildlife ranger. I cannot veer off course without written consent from the Director, and even if you are from wildlife," Shadrack pointed politely, "I would still need paperwork to do as you are asking."

Mark nodded, knowing he was wrong to ask the guide to make concessions. He knew the rule was, no civilians, the vehicle they were on was a private company, he would need to go to the wildlife office back in town, report the carnage and let those on duty there to investigate.

Shadrack swung the car towards the vultures. As he got closer he noticed a few predators lurking by. He eyed them cautiously but kept on course. After fifteen minutes, he slowed down to inspect the area. They were close. The stench testified to it. After a few bends, Shadrack stopped the vehicle. He raised his binoculars to his eyes and after a moment pointed, "There."

The trio followed his finger. There was a herd of dead buffaloes scattered in the bush.

Mark was on high alert. There were a few wild cats nearby.

"This looks disturbing," Shadrack said still in the safety of his vehicle. "Will have to call it in."

"Mmm, they look like those other buffalo we came to have a look at a year ago," Mark said, as he leaned over to have a closer look.

"Do you need to take a few samples?" Mpho turned to her husband

Mark shook his head. "We are not allowed, as Shadrack pointed. Government regulations. And even if we did have permission the decay has damaged any evidence we could have collected. I need to make a few calls," he huffed.

"Mmm, I will notify the officer on duty at the gate on our way out," Shadrack said, as he put the vehicle in first gear.

By the time the car parked back where they had been picked up, it was ten-thirty. Normally the excursion should take three hours, but the party had been unavoidably detained by the heap of dead buffalo.

The Painted Owl

"I HEAR THEY SAY THERE IS TSETSE FLY IN THE AREA," Venus was off her chair as soon as she saw Tori walk into her store.

"That is what the newspapers are saying," Tori waved the Guardian newspaper that was in her hand.

"You know, the disease comes from those countries up in the continent," Venus made a disgusted face. "This disease bore its ugly head around the nineteen twenties, as well as the nineteen sixties. Back then scientists had not come up with a better solution, so millions of wildlife and bush were destroyed in the attempt to get rid of the deadly pests."

"Wow, I never knew that the tik-tik could do that much damage!"

"Oh yes," Venus had made her way to the little kitchenette in her Painted Owl gift shop. She put the kettle on, placed two mugs on a tray together with tea bags, sugar, milk, and some biscuits. "I know you don't like the Tennis biscuits, so I got Choice Assorted this time," she smiled.

"Oh shame, you didn't have to do that," Tori felt guilty for not having thought of bringing something with her for them to share. She made a mental note to remember that the next time she visited.

"Your visits are the highlight of my week," the old lady chuckled as she dragged her feet back to her Amish Mission Style rocking chair.

Tori smiled warmly. "How is Gerald doing?"

"Oh, he is fine I guess. I haven't seen him all week. He keeps himself busy in his little nursery cum lab, some days he sleeps there."

"Oh, he has a nursery?"

"Yes, over the past couple of years he has taken to plants, especially fruit plants."

"You must have a number of oranges, mangos, and lemons in your yard. It saves you a lot of money."

"Gerald doesn't allow me to eat from his trees."

The comment made Tori uncomfortable so she swiftly changed the subject. "I was thinking of having you over again sometime soon."

Venus was thoughtful. "Why don't you come visit me? I can make us a nice super and if you are fortunate maybe my Gerald will take a shine to you and show you around his nursery."

"Oh wow, thank you. I will take you up on that offer."

There was a chime at the door. A few tourists walked in, amongst them, a Caucasian man with dreadlocks twisted in a slapdash manner. He wore this hairstyle with khaki pants, some flip flops, and a Bob Marley T-shirt. Tori was convinced that if the man were to speak, his accent would be an impersonation of someone of Caribbean descent, and if ever he were to be pulled into a debate about his style, he would say it was cultural appreciation and not appropriation. She watched as Venus engaged in good-natured banter with each tourist. Tori moved out of the way as they made payments and watched as the group moseyed about their day.

Venus wore a grin as she turned her attention back to Tori.

"Is it always this busy?"

"Yes, Kasane is never short of tourists. Because it is situated right at the corner of Botswana, an arm stretch away from three other countries, we get a bucket full of tourists each day."

"Very nice."

"How is your business coming along?" The old lady asked as she poured the hot water into the mugs.

"It's picking up again. I installed a pool a month back. So now that that project is done my guests have been trickling in again."

"Very good, I am glad your business is picking up. I love your independence Tori. I do ask myself several times in the day why you are single, but then I look at your achievements and think you are better off on your own, without someone dragging you down, and sallying you at every chance they get," Venus' face had hardened.

Tori could tell the conversation had taken a turn yet again so she tried to shift to a more positive light chatter. "Where do you get all your charming trinkets from?" she asked, taking a sip from the mug.

"Oh," Venus snapped back to her cheerful self. "There is a lady that comes by with a bunch of pictures of what she has. I am sure she buys stuff from Zambia, South Africa, Kenya, she is a big traveller, so she picks things up on her excursions."

"Cool."

"Then sometimes I get walk in's. Local artists, authors, and the like, there is a lady called Rose, she started a little company and makes handcrafted soap," Venus got up and walked to the soap display. "The lady is from Zambia, very talented. Look at this," Venus held out the soap to Tori.

"Wow, very impressive. Baobab Swirls," she shook her head as she read the tag on the bar of charcoal soap. She held the dark bar to her nose "smells glorious."

"Mmmhm, I sometimes use the soap myself. There is one made with donkey milk, goat milk, coffee, and cream, the woman is on a roll."

An idea suddenly popped into Tori's head. "Do you think you could possibly make an order for my lofts? I think these would work perfectly as little gifts for the guests when they arrive at the lofts."

"Yes, I can get more orders. You should also add earrings, for ladies, there are some lovely handmade earrings." Venus walked to the jewelry rack, "there are some really innovative people out there, here are some made from coke soda bottle tops, and then you have some made from safety pins." She said, handing them to Tori.

Tori walked over to the rack, her mind full of ideas. "I like this." Ever since she had installed the pool, he had been toying with the idea of increasing the accommodation. The grounds were immaculate, thanks to Small boy, and all three lofts were fully furnished, and beautifully dressed with ornaments, paintings, and potted indoor plants. "I think I like where you are going with this Venus. But what would I give the men?"

"Erm, let me see," Venus walked around her store, full of newfound energy. This deal would guarantee her regular income. She swirled a couple of shirts, paused for a second, and then dismissed them. She looked at some shoes, but then shook her head, "too expensive," finally she picked up key holders in one hand, and magnets in another. "What do you think of these?"

Tori walked over to Venus, she looked at the different key holders and magnets and decided on both. The deal was made. Tori would be getting a regular supply of handcrafted soap, fridge magnets, and key holders as little welcome gifts for her guests.

Monkey Business

Tori was pushing a trolley as she trotted to her car when she noticed a flyer on her windscreen. After plucking it from the clutches of the wipers she leaned over to glance at the license disk, it was expiring in two days.

"Rats! Will have to sort that out today," she whispered.

The post office was not as packed as she had thought it would be. Tori walked in and was welcomed by the guard stationed at the door.

"I am paying for the disc for my car," she announced.

"Okay," the man pointed to a line that was being assisted by a lady that looked like she needed to have a conversation with Dr. Nowzaradan from My 600 Pound Life. "You can join that line," he smiled.

After fifteen minutes, she was now next to be assisted. "Good morning," Tori smiled. "I have come to renew my disc."

The woman nodded.

Tori produced the car's particulars. After a few taps on the keyboard, the woman handed Tori back her documents, "Your car has been flagged. You need to go and pay the fine first before we can renew your license."

Tori frowned. "Flagged?" She didn't remember getting a ticket anywhere.

"You can go to the police station, they will help you," the woman suggested.

"Thank you," with a perplexed face, Tori walked out of the post office and made her way across the street to the police station. As she got near the station she noticed the baobab tree that Shadrack had mentioned on the safari she had enjoyed with Mpho and Mark. A few warthogs trotted by, which altered Tori's facial expression, but failed to alter her mood. She walked into the office, it looked somewhat abandoned. She looked around, walked out, then walked back in again, this time finding an officer by the counter with a plastic of magwinya (fat cakes) in one hand and a fresh cup of coffee, evident by the steam that was rising from the mug. "Dumelang," Tori greeted politely.

"Ee, le thusiwa jang?"

"Erm, I am just from the post office, I wanted to pay for my car disk, but the lady there said that I have been flagged. I just wanted to double-check if that is true. I don't remember getting charged for any traffic offenses."

"Mmhm," in a sloth-like manner, the man placed his mug down. He took a bite from his ligwinya, and started to talk with the piece of fried dough rolling around in his mouth. "Go to office number three. They will be able to help you there."

Tori thanked the man and walked through in search of office three. Upon locating office three, Tori knocked softly.

"Come in," a voice from the inside commanded.

Tori gently opened the door and trod lightly as she made her way to the man that seemed to be drowning in paperwork. "Dumelang."

"Ee, lekae," the man muttered without raising his eyes to meet Tori's.

Tori wondered if she should relay her predicament to the man, or wait for him to give her his full attention. She stood quietly, afraid to even take a seat.

After five minutes the man exhaled, "Yes, mma. How can I help you?"

Tori perked up. "I was at the post office, trying to pay for my license disc, but the lady there told me I had been flagged. I don't remember being charged, so I just wanted to double-check what the issue is."

"Mhm, what is the plate number for the car?"

Tori gave him the number. The man punched the numbers on the computer. "Mhm, looks like you owe one thousand pula in Letlhakane," the man said pointing at the screen.

"Letlhakane?"

"Yes, la Orapa."

"Uhu! I have never been to that side. Does it say what you charged me with? When did this take place?"

"Erm," the man lowered his glasses and rolled the chair closer to the screen. "It says, Mphoeng Mosupiemang. Did you lend your car to him around May this year?"

Tori's mouth went dry. "May, Letlhakane, Mphoeng. This doesn't make sense. In May I was here, freezing my butt off constructing the lofts that are up in Plateau. I was there every single day of the build. I was nowhere near Letlhakane. I even have eye witnesses."

"What about this Mphoeng character? Maybe you lent him your car."

"That is impossible."

"Mmm, explain."

Tori shifted on her seat and in a low tone she divulged that she was living in her Surf during the time of the build.

The man gave Tori a quizzical glare. "O raya jang o re living in your car?"

"I didn't know anyone in Kasane, and I could not find suitable accommodation, so I used an empty BHC house and lived there till the project was done."

The man bellowed with laughter. "He picked up his phone still in tears and dialed a few numbers. "Hello, mmm, ke mang?"

Tori could hear the voice on the other end of the line. "Ke Kobole,"

"Ehe, nna ke mang?"

"Ga ke itse?"

"No monna, you must know who I am, you know this voice."

"Erm, no, I don't know who you are," the voice on the other end insisted.

"Comfort here monna, hashtag Comfortability," the man bragged.

Tori pressed her upper and lower lip together to suppress a cackle.

"Give me Tidimalo," he continued. The line went quiet. Another voice was heard.

"Hello?"

"Yes monna Tidimalo, ke na le a lady here, he has been flagged, and the name is of a person she doesn't know. He needs to pay her license disk which expires soon. Please can you assist?"

Tori was appalled by the man's misuse of the he/she pronouns.

"Yes, erm, she needs to write an affidavit stating her case. After that, you need to scan that affidavit and send it through to us."

The man made a face, "eish, we don't have a scanner waitse," he turned to a dead scanner that was at the corner of the room. "Can I WhatsApp you the document?"

"Yes, that should be fine."

"Okay, let me do that now."

After hanging up, Comfortability glared at Tori, his glasses at the edge of his fleshy nose. "Erm, o utlule akere?"

Tori possed dumb.

"He says you need to write an affidavit."

Tori bopped her head.

"Here," he handed Tori an affidavit form, "Jaanong oa go kwalela kae?"

Tori looked straight at the man, "I will use the edge of your desk, I can write it right here."

The man brushed his nose. "Okay, ee, write," he commanded.

After Tori was done, she handed the sheet of paper to the man. He browsed through her statement and nodded before picking up his phone so he could take a picture and send it through to the officer in Letlhakane.

"Eish," the man fidgeted with the phone and eventually gave up, "there is a bit of a shadow every time I try to take a picture."

"Would you like me to scan the document for you and WhatsApp it to you, and then you can forward it to the officer in Letlhakane?"

"Scan it how, there is no scanner here." Each word he uttered sounded like it were being clubbed.

Tori pulled out her phone, clicked on a scanning app before silently scanning the affidavit. She proceeded to request Comfort's cell number and sent him the scanned document.

Comfort leaned back on his office chair, with an impressed expression glued to his face. He tapped on his phone and forwarded the document to the man in Letlhakane. "Aaaah!" He exclaimed, "I forgot to put a stamp on the affidavit." He pulled out the stamp, and then banged the sheet of paper as though he were nailing it to the desk. "Okay, scan again and send."

Tori obeyed. After sending the stamped affidavit to hashtag

Comfortability, she gazed at his phone. It vibrated. The man picked it up and smiled. Using his porky thumbs, he clicked the screen and waited.

"Mhm, blue tick, he should have it done in a minute."

Tori nodded gratefully.

"So, ware you were building lofts?"

"Yes."

"What is a loft mme gone?"

"Oh. They are basically double storey buildings, but the top part is done a little differently, there are no walls that overlook the bottom floor." Tori scrolled through her phone and showed the man the lofts, from the beginning of them being constructed till what they looked like now with the garden taking shape.

"Wow, this is BEAUTIFUL!"

Tori smiled proudly, "thank you."

"Mmm, ke bona le the dates of the pictures, nyaya tota you were not in Letlhakane." Comfort's phone started to vibrate. "Mhm... let us check if it is reflecting on this end," he spoke as he tapped his phone screen. He moved the mouse around, and from the way he kept banging it on his desk, Tori figured it was a faulty mouse. "Ehe," he punched a few keys with his index fingers. "Eh! Helang batho, ke dirile eng! No, no, no, I can't accept," the man had both hands on the back of his square head.

"What is it?" Tori was on the edge of her seat.

"I must have pressed something, it wants me to accept un-flagging you."

"But isn't that what we want?"

"No no, they have to do it in Letlhakane. Let me see." He leaned forward, and using his right index finger punched a few keys. "Ehe, I fixed it. Eish, I almost put myself in hot soup."

Tori let out a sigh of contained frustration.

The man banged the mouse on the desk again before shaking it on the wooden desk. He clicked a few times, then sat back again. "Amin? Where is that surname from?"

"Molepolole."

"So you are originally from Molepolole?"

"Ee rra."

"Mhm, and your parents?"

"Ba tswa Molepolole. Well, my dad is from there, my mother ke mokalaka."

"Ehe, oa se eitse sekalaka?"

"Ee rra?"

"O serious?"

"Yes, I am serious."

"Mmeabo ba no dwa ngai kanyi?"

"Siviya."

"Ehe?"

"Wa ngina ngai ikwele?"

"Ku Maun, University nda nginila ku South Africa."

"Mhm…" he shook his head, impressed by Tori's accent, pure Kalanga, no English or Indian twang to it.

Comfortability's phone vibrated. He swiped the screen with his stubby fingers and fought with the mouse yet again. "Ehe. Wonderful. You are in the clear. Ba go flagolotse."

Tori let out a sigh of relief. "Thank you so much!"

The man printed out two copies of the document which proved that indeed Tori's vehicle had been un-flagged. "Here you go, madam."

"Thank you so much!" Tori beamed, as she snatched the document from his rotund fingers.

"Yah, tell them there at the post office that rre Comfort, a.k.a Comfortability assisted you and that ga o na molato," he smiled, proud of his achievement.

Tori pursed her lips together as she backed out of the office and charged for the post office.

By the time Tori got home she was hot and bothered. It had been a long and hard day. As she approached the kitchenette to unpack the groceries, she noticed that something was amiss. Leading to the glass door out back there was a trail of debris. As she followed it, she noticed that the trail diverted its course ending at a small window on the left side of the building. "Monkeys," she whispered. "Ugh, Lesedi must have forgotten to close this window when she left," she huffed. There was broken glass everywhere, the monkeys had found their way to the glass container that housed the sugar. There were granules all over the place. The bowl she usually kept full of fruits and vegetables was empty. Bits and pieces of onions were scattered everywhere. "Monkey's like onions?" She muttered as she walked to the cleaning cupboard to find the dustpan.

Halfway through cleaning up, Tori's phone rang. It was her mother.

"Hey Beatrice, long time," she exhaled.

Pause.

"Monkeys have been in my house, and have made a mess. Let me put you on loudspeaker as I clean up."

Her mother's voice filled the room. "How are things on your end?"

"Fine."

"You don't sound fine."

"I just had a long day, that's all."

"What Happened?"

"Ah, I had to renew my car disc. Went to the post office and they said I had a charge that had not been paid for, so I crossed over to the police station. Met a guy called Comfort, who referred to himself as 'Comfortability'."

"What!" Tori's mother roared on the other end of the phone.

"Exactly. Something that should have taken me at least thirty minutes ended up taking half the day. I just walked into my house and found the monkeys had been in. The lady that cleans must have forgotten to close the window. Well, I know she did, because the small window was ajar."

"Shame," Beatrice had stopped laughing.

"And I know the ice cream has melted. So I'm going to have milkshake ice cream,"

"Ao batho," you could hear Beatrice was tempted to laugh again but held it together.

"So when are you and Dad coming over? I have been inviting you and you have been postponing for almost a year now. Batho ba kwano probably think I don't have parents."

"Eish, I know we haven't really lived up to our word. I am thinking we may come at the end of next month. Will you be available?"

"Mom, I am always available for my parents."

"Awww, sweet. Would you like us to bring anything when we come?"

"No. Not really."

"Mmm, we may fly. Driving all the way to Kasane also is a job and a half, by the time you get there you need a day to recover just from the drive up."

"Okay, I am looking forward to having you over."

Beatrice paused.

"What is it, mother?" Tori knew what her mother was going to ask.

"So, I was wondering if you have found him yet?"

"I wasn't aware I was searching for Wally." Tori teased. She had resorted to her mother's determined search of a husband for her as finding Wally. A character found in Martin Handford's illustrations that challenged readers to find Wally who was dressed in a striped red and white sweater hidden in a throng of people. "When I do find a random guy stuck in between an ice cream truck and a herd of elephants in strips in Kasane I will give you a shout," she chuckled.

"Tori, ke serious. Your father and I worry about you."

"What is there to worry about Ma, I am a successful business lady, why do you think I need a man to fulfill me?"

"Because that is how we were designed."

"I'll call you later Mother, let me finish cleaning up and take a shower."

"Sure, keep your eyes peeled for your Wally hon," Beatrice teased back.

Tori rolled her eyes and hung up.

Her memory took her back to when she was at University.

"Ma, I aced my exams today."

"Well done. Have you told your father?"

"No, not yet. I just got the results. You are the first person I thought to call."

"Sweet, keep your little nose in those books. I know you will do well."

"Thanks, mom. How are Ishaan and Ryan?"

"You want to tell me you still haven't checked on your brothers yet?"

"Ah, we really don't have much in common."

"Erm, your father and I caught up with them recently… They seem to be doing well."

"Mmm, and dad? Anyways I will call him after and tell him about my exams."

"Okay, dear,"

There was a pregnant pause.

"What is it, mom?"

"Why do you think there is something?"

"When you pause like that I know you want to ask me something but are thinking of the right word so you can tread lightly."

Beatrice could be heard laughing on the other end of the line. "Well, now that you ask. I was just wondering if you found something?"

"LIKE WHAT?"

"Something like what?"

"You know, someone. A guy friend maybe?"

"I didn't come to Rhodes to find a husband ma!" Tori said in frustration.

"I know, I know," Tori could hear that her mother was walking on eggshells. "But you know I worry about you. Your brothers don't seem to have a problem finding women to be friends with."

"Well I do have women that are my friends," she teased.

"Tori… you know what I mean."

Tori slowly exhaled some breath through her nose in an attempt to calm herself. She could feel her blood starting to boil. This topic was one her mother had always casually popped up in eeeeeevery conversation ever since her bust had protruded in her early teens. The only thing that she was grateful for was that her parents did not believe in arranged marriages. What her mother did believe in though was matchmaking.

"Mmmm," her mother was thoughtful, "I hope since your exams are now over, you will be more active in the search?"

"I tell you what mom, you will be the first to know as soon as I find Wally."

"Don't joke."

Tori let out a little laugh. She knew her mother meant well. She also knew that the pressure was not really coming from her mother but from the overbearing relatives on her father's side. Ever since Tori's father had married her mother, Beatrice could do nothing right. At family gatherings, Beatrice was always on edge. She didn't know how to make samosas the right way, she didn't know how to make chapattis correctly. Her curry was not spicy enough. Her clothes were too western. Her children had lost their culture. Tori noticed that at each gathering her father shielded and stood up for her mother. And at times Beatrice would come up with excuses not to go to family shindigs.

"Mma, I will find someone at my own pace," Tori reassured softly.

"Okay love."

Tori could hear the slight frustration in her mother's voice. "I will call you again soon, say hi to dad for me."

"Okay, darling. Take care."

All her conversations with her mother while Tori had been at university had always had a little nudge on finding a match. When Tori had failed to produce a male companion by the end of her second year, uncle Vikash had been summoned. Tori was invited to several family gatherings, and at each one there had been one or two potential men. By the time Tori completed varsity, she had been introduced to more than twenty eligible bachelors of Asian descent. None had tempted Tori.

"Are you sure you are not batting for the same team?" Beatrice had giggled to her only daughter one day.

Tori was mortified at the thought. "What does that mean mama?"

"I mean, are you sure you have feelings for, you know, men?"

"Of course I do Mma!" Tori shook her head in disbelief.

"This is a serious matter, my child. When was the last time you dated?" Beatrice had put on a serious face.

"Erm…" The truth was that Tori had never been in any serious relationships. The boys from her primary and high school were all just close friends. She had never thought anything more of them. She remembered there was one guy, though, while she was at boarding school that she had had a crush on, but nothing had ever blossomed. While at Rhodes, Tori had immersed herself in her studies. Socializing and dating had been of no interest to her. She had a few crushes here and there, but not strong enough to propel her to profess her undying love to anyone. "A month back, but it only lasted a week," she lied.

Once she had obtained her degree and was back in Botswana, her mother had made it her sole purpose to find her only daughter a husband. Beatrice was determined to do something right so that the Amin family would finally accept her. Every weekend, there was a gathering at their house; Beatrice never failed to invite a Dewan, a Chandra, a Kumar, a Ray, or a Thakor. All were charming and well-mannered, but still not tempting enough for Tori to relinquish her freedom.

Now, as she sat on the patio watching the crisp water in the pool she had recently installed, she couldn't help but smile. She found she was happy. Happy at the prospect of a new life even further away from her overbearing, but well-meaning mother who was determined to find a man that would be chained to her till death do them apart by hoops of steel. She had a dream, and she was at the cusp of realizing that dream. Peter's Place was just the beginning.

!XÓÕ

THE MAN WAS BESIDE HIMSELF with pain. The more he wiggled the tighter the irate animal would bite. There was a group of able-bodied men from the !Xóõ speaking tribe tediously helping as hard as they could to try and release the gentleman from the unsympathetic tight clutch the honey badger was currently inflicting on the bawling twenty-five-year-old.

To Mr. White, the wild was his second wife and third child. He enjoyed the nomadic lifestyle. Every opportunity he could find, he spent camping. Deep down he believed life in the bush was what he was born for. Every opportunity he got was used on excursions. He would pack minimal luggage, bid farewell to his wife before charging out into what the unrelenting wild Botswana had to offer; whether it was in the semi-arid sandy region of the Kalahari, or the marshlands of the Savuti. Anywhere where he could pitch a tent was the perfect location for Mr. White to study the vast species Botswana had tucked away in its backyard. Rare and exotic was what he reveled in, from insects to birds, mammals to reptiles. It was a passion. Others though would categorize it as mania.

The man had spent many a year in the bustling town of Francistown that had a high density of folks from the Kalanga tribe. He believed his neighbours to be cretins. Having no sense of how to handle or even rear animals, whether they were Orpington chickens or terriers. "Humans are clueless," he reasoned, unyielding to the idea of standing by and watching as novices botched the job. Any opportunity he got he would rescue "abandoned" or "mistreated" dogs, cats, sheep, chickens, and many more house pets. If there was a dangerous animal in the vicinity, he would always insist that he be summoned so he could assist in removing the animal and rehabilitating it in a new and safe environment. "The Department of Wildlife is clueless," he would grunt.

He had been living amongst the !Khong tribe who spoke ⊠ta', for a little over six months. During that time, Mr. White had picked up some of the dialect that consisted of clicking sounds. They were an indigenous people, a red people, gentle, kind, with an intimate knowledge of the land. White's interest was their hunting techniques. The San did not value firearms, their way of stalking game had been practiced for hundreds of years; these were the techniques Mr. White was keenly interested in. The women of the tribe were of no consequence to him, all they did all day was sing, make jewelry, cook, and forage. The svelte men, red rind mimicking the dead skin on their bodies, embodied all that White wanted to be. He had exchanged his western clothes for the animal skin that the tribe was garbed in, conveniently forgetting how relentless the Botswana sun was. Within a day he had burnt to a crisp, his sensitive skin taking the colouring of a pig, raw and painful. It took the women in the tribe almost three weeks nursing his hide with medicinal plants. They would chew the roots, or bulbs, till soft, before gently smearing the saliva laced porridge-like mixture on his sensitive skin. Once White was fully recovered he reasoned that the dead skin would act as protection from the sun's rays. His goal was to try and get his complexion as close to his newfound family as possible.

Over the six months, he had spent with the tribe, White had learned how to make a traditional bow and arrow. He was skilled in concocting poison, tracking wildebeest, avoiding predators, and stealing ostrich eggs. One morning, the head of the settlement announced at dinner around the fire that White would be accompanying the men on a hunt the next day. Excitement was in the air. That night the women danced and sang into the night. White spent the night looking up at the ceiling of the grass hut that had been constructed for him after he had abandoned his four-season tent which he had purchased at Haskins in Francistown.

Before sunrise the next day White heard the call. He got up to follow the sound. He picked up the bow and reed-shafted arrows he had helped prepare the day before, carefully making sure that the tip of the arrows that were smeared in poison could not lance him in any way as it would mean death with no hope of an antidote to reverse the damage. He smiled as he thought back on how he had been given the privilege of assisting in the poison making. After weeks and weeks of watching on the sidelines as younger members of the tribe made the fatal substance, he finally was deemed eligible to be a part of the ritual. He had assisted with gathering the ingredients. White had watched carefully as the elder of the tribe scraped and pounded the seeds from the poisonous berries that had been collected, then he carefully squeezed the guts out of a toxic beetle after slicing its head off before finally chewing the root of a Sansevieria, careful not to swallow the juices as the root contained powerful toxins. The man then slowly mixed the three ingredients together, being mindful not to spill any as this would be a waste. All the hunters at the camp had their arrows on hand. When the mixture was ready, they methodically smeared each metallic tip with the poison, after which they laid the arrows to bake in the sun. These were the arrows that White now carried as he went to answer the call for the hunt in the wee hours of the morning.

Four shadows huddled at the corner of the camp. The head hunter Xao made a few clicking sounds, two men, one with a protruding stomach and another young and lean, nodded. White also fell in line and complied with the instructions. Xao pointed east and started to run. The other three followed him closely, with only the stars and the moon as luminaries. White was at the back of the pack. After thirty minutes of running, they reached a shallow waterhole; the water had been receding quickly due to the high temperatures and lack of rain. Xao signaled with his hands. There were a handful of hartebeests scattered around the water source. At Xao's signal the three hunters, including White, scattered to form a V formation. White was on Xao's tail, while the other two moved stealthily on the left. As White cautiously kept his eye on Xao moving stealthily close to his path, he stumbled on what he thought was a root. He lurched to regain stability and found that the root had grown a ferocious temper and was attacking him. He quietly tried to fight back, shooing the animal, but to no avail. The ratel, identified by its voetsek attitude, vicious attacks, and large chip on its shoulder; has been known to assault lions, puff adders, hyenas, leopards, cobras, buffalo, and many other animals that are twice, even three times their size. It was now relentlessly attached to Mr. White refusing to back down. He knew to stay clear of this black predator with white stripes, but on this early morning, he had missed the signal from Xao to stay clear of its path resulting in him stumbling right into it. As White wrestled with the creature, he remembered the urban legend surrounding the honey badger. It was known for notoriously emasculating its prey. As White fought back, he made sure the meter-long mammal with its stubby feet and long claws could not reach his upper legs. He had heard once around the campfire, how the honey badger had dismembered a buffalo's testicles a year earlier. He was determined not to become the first human to be documented as the first too.

The solitary hunter found a soft spot on White's right leg and dug its teeth in. White had tried not to make a sound in fear of startling the prey, yet the savage on his heels was making enough noise for the both of them. He was beside himself with pain. The more he wiggled the tighter the irate animal would bite. Xao and the other two hunters, on hearing the commotion, abandoned their posts and ran to White's aid tirelessly trying to loosen the grip of the unsympathetic tight clutch the honey badger had on this bawling new hunter.

Cresta Mowana

THE AROMA OF BOILING SAUCES and rice wafted through the air. Tori walked into the beautifully laid-out hotel. There was a majestic baobab tree in the center of the premises, as her eyes floated beyond it they were met by the Chobe. She smiled as she took in the luxury that had been prepared for tourists from all walks of life. She headed for the upstairs bar to her left, a little oasis she had discovered a year and a half ago when she had been temporarily homeless, living out of her car like a hobo. Happy hour was indeed happy. Tori ordered a rum shooter. As she took a sip of the lovingly prepared drink, she could taste the coffee liqueur as it trickled down her throat.

"Is that all madam?" the barman asked.

"No," Tori tilted her head as though to say, "as if that is all I am having…" She glanced at the menu and ordered the meal that was on special. "I will also have a Spanish Coffee, please."

The man nodded and went to work. Tori smiled at the barman before walking towards the edge of the balcony that overlooked the vast waters. She found a vacant oversized rattan straw lounge chair and threw herself on it. The view was breathtaking; the noises, hearty laughter mingled with the singing of wild birds, and hippos that were lounging in the murky water.

Tori watched as a couple walked along the pathway oblivious to her intrusive glare. Palm fronds on the ground, a few impalas skipping about; the perfect scene. A feeling of longing suddenly tugged at her. The feeling was interrupted by the barman, he handed Tori her Spanish Coffee before rushing back to his post. A few people were trickling in. Tori didn't care to engage in any small talk. Soft indie folk music was playing.

"Hey... I thought it was you."

Tori tilted her head and found herself gazing into emerald green eyes. She almost choked on her drink as she sat up straight. "Hi, what a surprise," she gulped, looking around for Gabe's girlfriend.

"How have you been?" he said, taking a seat next to her.

"Well. I have been well."

"Are you visiting again?"

"Oh, no... I live here now." Every word was excruciatingly uncomfortable.

"Oh yes, you mentioned before at that place that one time." Gabe scrambled for the memory, but couldn't find it.

"The bottle store," Tori assisted. The memory had been seared in her brain for eternity. She remembered how she had squirmed in his presence, the exact way she was squirming now.

"Oh yes, the bottle store," Gabe smiled. "Why did you decide to move here?"

A waiter appeared with Tori's food. Tori gave Gabe a look, "Sorry I had ordered something before you came."

"That's okay, I've ordered something myself." Gabe turned his attention to the waiter, "if you don't mind bringing my order here please."

The man nodded and swiftly gaited for the stairs.

Gabe's piercing eyes were pinned on Tori.

"Sorry, what was the question again?" she adjusted, trying to find the right angle to sit comfortably.

"Why did you move to Kasane?"

"Oh, I love it here. The first time I saw it I loved it."

"Mmm, funny, same," Gabe said, his gaze intensifying.

Tori took a sip from her drink before offering some food to Gabe. She was starving, yet is presence was making her stomach churn. She knew she would not be able to hold any of the food down. "Yah?" she gazed at the guests that kept filling the room. "I settled here because it is a wonderful place. What this town offers, you will never find anywhere else in the world."

"Mmm, I must say Kasane is a gem. How are your friends doing?" Gabe changed the subject. "The ones you were here with that time?"

"Fine, they visited recently actually, a couple of months back. They are doing well."

"You heard there is a tsetse fly outbreak?"

"Well it is not an outbreak anymore, they have handled the situation," Tori corrected. "Well, that is what Mark said the last time we spoke."

"Mmhm. I didn't notice any spraying," Gabe commented.

"No, they used a different technique this time round; Mark explained it to me, now I have forgotten. Something to do with introducing male flies, somehow they reduce the female flies since female flies are the ones that are hosts."

Gabe frowned.

"Yah, I don't understand it. He did explain it. But because I couldn't understand how that works, I am doing a bad job convincing you that they have sorted the situation."

"Mmk, whatever you say," he smiled, sipping his beer.

After Gabe's food arrived, Tori found it a little easier to nibble at hers. She ordered a refill of er drink and a little dessert.

"So where does one find you, Tori?"

Tori shot a look at Gabe. "Find me? Are you planning on losing me?" she teased.

"No, I mean, where do you live, or where can I contact you so I can hang out with you?"

"Erm. I stay up in Plateau. But why would you want to hang out with me? I thought you had a lady friend that you hang out with already! I scanned the room earlier, actually wondering why she wasn't hanging on your shoulder."

"Who are you talking about?" Gabe asked, a bewildered look on his face.

"The lady at the liquor store, your bae?"

Gabe choked on his beer causing the beer to spill out of his nostrils. He gasped for air before finally coughing. Tori quickly gave him a napkin and patted his back.

He finally let out a little smile, between little coughs. "What are you talking about?"

"Your girlfriend!" Tori pressed.

"Did someone tell you that she was my girlfriend? Is there a rumor floating about that I am not aware of?"

"No," Tori shook her head quickly. "I just assumed that day that you were together. You mentioned that she was your partner." Her shoulders dropped as she wondered if she had heard him wrong.

"Ohhhh… She is my partner, at work, she flies as well. We were sent to Kasane together, and so technically, she is my partner." Now he was laughing violently.

Tori was getting embarrassed as Gabe's laughter was drawing unwanted eyes in their direction. "It's not that funny," she retorted.

"Yes it is, actually," he giggled.

"Well, my mistake then."

"And you, why isn't that guy from that time hanging on your shoulder?"

"You mean Glen, why should he be?"

"Well, the guy was clearly into you."

"That's a shame."

"So you are not into him?"

"He is a nice guy, but..."

As Tori was talking Gabe leaned over and kissed her cheek and quickly nodded goodbye. Tori sat there for a few minutes bewildered before she turned to see where he had disappeared to. Tori scanned the room to see what could have prompted him to leave so abruptly, and then got to her feet to run after him. By the time she got to the lobby, the man had vanished into thin air.

As she got out of the shower back at Peter's Place, loft number three, she couldn't help but touch her cheek. She could still feel him. She shook her head as though trying to shed the sensation. "I wonder what could have startled him," she whispered as she snuggled into bed. That night she dreamt of Gabe.

The next morning Tori saddled onto her two thousand and eight Surf and headed for Cresta Mowana. The lounge was a different scene from the night before. She walked up to the barman and apologized. "I realized when I got home that I left last night without paying my bill."

The barman smiled. "Yes ma'am, I remember you. He tapped on the screen in front of him and produced a bill. Tori handed the man her card but he raised his hand. "The gentleman you were with last night settled the bill.

"Oh?" Tori was bewildered. The man had scurried out of the room so quickly, when did he settle the bill she wondered.

"Are you staying for breakfast? "The barman gently enquired.

"I might as well," she smiled sheepishly.

The bartender's face exploded into a smile. "There is a buffet down at the restaurant."

The restaurant was grand. There was ample seating. The room

was erected with the views in mind. The floor-to-ceiling doors, and wide windows brought sufficient light, as well as the outdoors in. You felt like you were a part of nature as you enjoyed your mimosa. Tori walked up to the serving stations and fed her eyes before feeding her belly. There was 'sweet' on one end and 'savory' on the other end. Tori's palate was craving for something salty. She reached for one of the plates, as she did, another hand reached for the same plate.

"Oh, sorry," she recoiled, allowing the person to pick the plate.

"Uhu, Tori!"

Tori followed the limb that had grabbed the plate before her and found herself staring at Bastian. Tori shook her head. "You need to stop bumping into me like this."

"Should I?" He teased resulting in Tori blushing.

"Visiting again?"

"Kasane calls me every year."

"Does it?"

"Yah, and you? I saw you close to two years ago. I thought you were going to visit me in Jwaneng, what happened?"

Tori picked a few bacon strips with the pair of tongs that were placed in the serving dish. "Well, I didn't have time to come visit."

"How come?"

"I live in Kasane now. I had a project that took all my attention. I didn't have a minute to think of myself."

"Is it?"

"Yah."

The pair had completed picking their preferences and were making their way to the juice dispenser. Tori poured herself a cup of orange juice and Sebastian followed suit.

"Do you mind if I join you for breakfast?" Sebastian asked as he followed Tori around the room.

"Sure, where did you want to sit?"

"Outside looks nice, there are some chairs out there overlooking the river."

"Okay," Tori led the way and chose a secluded spot for them to enjoy their meals.

Palm fronds were scattered on the grass below. One could spot bushbuck grazing. A few birds swooped across. A soft breeze tickled the fringes of hair on Tori's neck. She took a generous sip from her freshly squeezed citrus juice. Sebastian took a hungry bite from the croissant he had dished out for himself.

"So you live here, what do you do?" Sebastian asked between chews.

"I am retired," Tori smiled.

"At your age? No!" Sebastian shook his head in disbelief.

"Seriously though, I love it here. I run a small business that helps pay the bills, and the rest of my days I spend exploring what this part of Botswana has to offer."

"Wow, sounds like you are living the dream!"

"Honestly, I won't lie to you. I pinch myself every day when I wake up. From the time I came to visit, that time when we bumped into each other, I could not stop thinking of this place. So I made plans to move here."

"Well, I must say Kasane looks good on you."

Tori blushed as she took another sip from her juice. A waiter hovered by, Tori gestured for more juice, while Sebastian opted for some coffee.

"Why are you back in Kasane?"

"Work."

"Oh. I didn't know Debswana had people working in Kasane."

"Nah, not for them. For a personal thing, I am pursuing."

"Oh, is it? Care to share?"

"It's still under wraps, maybe one day I will share," he smiled coyly.

Tori fell silent. She was enjoying the company as well as the food, the scenery was breathtaking and the service, top class.

"How come we never dated back then?"

The question hit Tori like a ton of bricks. She acted as though she hadn't been frazzled by it. "Well," she cleared her throat. "I don't see how we could have dated, to be honest."

"Why do you say that?"

"It was against the rules."

"Everyone was doing it."

What Sebastian failed to notice was that Tori was referring to the rules set by her parents, rules that were steeped in culture.

"Well, what is the point of looking back on those days with great nostalgia? They are days gone by, we might as well focus on the present," Tori whispered.

"Are you free next Friday? Not this coming Friday, but the following Friday. I'd like to take you on a little picnic."

Tori smiled. "I will make myself available."

Sundowners

Tori's parents arrived late in the evening on a Tuesday afternoon. They had packed lightly. Dressed in matching safari outfits, the pair looked cute in a silly way. She walked up to her father and kissed him on the cheek before hugging him, before doing the same with her mother.

"How have you been?"

"Well, well," her father smiled.

"Good. I can't wait to show you around," the excitement in Tori's voice was apparent. She took a hold of her parent's luggage and pushed it into the back of her car.

"Why haven't you gotten a better vehicle?" her father wrinkled his nose as though he had just inhaled a bad smell.

"Roxi has been good to me. The reason I got her is so I can go camping, and do some safari trips. I can't exactly use a luxurious car in the bush."

"Erm, you can," her father pushed, causing Tori to roll her eyes.

"I'd rather spend my money on other things, Dad," she stressed firmly. "I like my car, and I don't have any intentions of exchanging her for anything else," Tori found she was already getting annoyed with her father five minutes into their stay.

"You know, I can't remember the last time your father and I were in Kasane," Beatrice changed the subject. "It has changed. Not too much though."

"Mmhm," Tori was not interested in being pulled into her mother's small talk. She drove in silence till they reached the lofts.

"Is this it, this is amazing! glorious!" Beatrice was impressed as she got out of the vehicle. "Darling," she looked at Tori, "I am so proud of you!" She walked over to where Tori was standing and gave her a kiss on the cheek.

Tori felt her mood lighten a bit. Her mother's enthusiasm was infectious. She smiled reluctantly as she offloaded her parent's luggage.

"It is nice," her father grunted.

"Thank you," Tori said, still in a sulk.

Beatrice walked around the premises, her face bright, proud eyes and a wide grin. "Who does your garden?"

"Oh, I designed it myself, but I have a guy that comes in and maintains the place, he is supposed to be here actually. Maybe he is outback. Tori walked to the urban wood pivot door that had glass on each side, she turned the key and pushed. As she walked into the loft she had made into a home, she couldn't help but be enveloped by a sense of pride. She had had so many visitors; tourists and friends to the loft, but none of them evoked as much emotion as her parents did. She wanted them to love her work. She wanted them to admire, to be proud, and to give her a stamp of approval. Their opinion meant more to her than all the reviews she had gotten on TripAdvisor. She walked up to the bedroom and placed their suitcases on the floor in her walk-in closet.

"Honey?" Beatrice called from downstairs.

Tori answered the call by promptly going down the stairs. "Yes, Mom?"

"Oh, I was just looking at your backyard. This is marvelous!" Beatrice was standing by the window, gazing through the glass windows that led outback. The pool was sparkling clean, and the ground immaculately manicured. There were a few bushbuck and warthogs grazing just beyond the electric fence.

Tori smiled as she opened the fridge. She pulled the plate of hors d'oeuvres she had prepared and filled two glasses of her mom and dad's favourite wine. "Mmm, here you go," she said as she served her parents. After they had picked up their drinks and dipped a few crackers in the homemade hummus she had blended to submission, Tori rolled open the glass door that led to the backyard. A gush of inviting wind swooped into the house. "You can make yourselves comfortable." she smiled as she walked back to the kitchenette to pour herself some shandy.

The three sat on the terrace, enjoying each other's company. Tori's father seemed to have relaxed his shoulders a bit.

"You have done a good job here my dear daughter," her father muttered stiffly. His words of endearment always sounded awkward and somewhat rehearsed.

Beatrice smiled at her husband and gave a nod of approval.

Tori had put together a little itinerary for her parents. She started off with a visit to Victoria Falls, then a game drive with Dusk till Dawn, and finally a boat cruise on the four-seater boat owned by the same company.

"I forgot how tranquil being on a cruise like this is."

"Yah, it's one of my favourite things to do," Tori inhaled taking in the full scope of the Chobe.

"So..." Beatrice said after slugging down a crisp cold Savanna Dry. "Any news of Waldo?"

"Mother..." Tori whispered.

"I mean, Kasane must be a large catchment area for such Waldo's, or is it Wally?"

Tori noticed that the drink had gone straight to her mother's head.

"It's Wally, Mom," Tori rolled her eyes.

"Who is this Wally?" Tori's father asked curiously.

"Oh, it's nothing, Mom just likes to tease me," Tori skirted.

"No, I am not teasing," Beatrice said, signaling to the guide to pop open another Savannah for her. "I want my daughter to get married. She is successful. Has the brains, is beautiful, and is single. Ludicrous!" the woman slurred.

"Beatrice, leave the child alone."

"Thanks, Dad."

"No, Pravin. I refuse to sit back and watch my child's womb shrivel up into dust."

"Really, Mother?"

"Why haven't you found anyone, huh?" The alcohol had dissolved any sugar-coating Beatrice was accustomed to using when she touched on the topic.

"I just haven't found anyone yet."

"Hogwash!"

"Beatrice!" Pravin reprimanded.

"You better back me on this Pravin, help me or you will regret it," Beatrice's eyes had gone buck wild.

Tori's father looked at his child sympathetically and raised his hands. He got up from where he had been sitting and moved closer to his daughter who was conveniently sitting next to the cooler box. He slowly opened the box, got himself a beer, and a packet of biltong.

"Don't you try and ignore me Pravin!" Beatrice was now on a roll.

Tori turned to look at her father, who was chowing violently on some ostrich biltong.

"Are you even interested in starting a family?"

"Erm," Tori knew that when her mother was in this mood, there was no deterring her till she got the answers she needed. Whether the answers were pleasant or not was of no consequence, the issue was getting to the bottom of the matter.

"Spit it out," she spat.

Feeling nailed to a corner, Tori decided to call a spade a spade. "I am not attracted to Asian men."

Pravin shot his daughter a questionable glare.

"And what is wrong with Asian?" Beatrice was on her daughter like a mad cat.

"I mean, there are many attractive men who are Asian, you introduced me to a large number of them," Tori tried to joke. Neither her mother nor her father was smiling. "But," she put back on her serious face. "I am just not attracted to them."

"And who are you attracted to?" It was her father asking.

His question sent a chill down Tori's spine. She took a long sip from her glass of wine and cleared her throat. "Other races," she said under her breath.

"Speak up child!" Beatrice was irritable.

"Other races," she said a little louder. She dragged another sip from her glass before she continued. "I am attracted to black and white, blue and yellow men, dad. I shouldn't be forced only to marry Asians, I should have the freedom to choose anyone, of any race that is compatible with me, and that has the same values that I hold dear."

"I won't allow it!" Pravin boomed.

Tori's eyes squinted as she looked at her father. "Isn't that a little hypocritical, considering that you married a black woman? You made your choice, regardless of race and color," she said pointing at her mother.

"That is different."

"Why, because you are a man and you can do whatever you want, and I, being female, need to be dictated to?" The sass in her tone was very apparent.

"You do as you are told, young lady!" Pravin tried to regain dominance.

Beatrice was mute, watching at a distance as she pumped herself full of her drink.

Tori shook her head, "Nah. This is not a dictatorship. I will choose to live my life the way I want. I have been living in fear of this very topic my whole life. Mom, thank you for insisting on addressing the elephant in the room, it's high time we had this conversation. I want to date. I have wanted to date for such a long time. But I have always been afraid of what you will say. Always afraid of your disapproval. But I don't need your approval anymore. I am a big girl. I can choose who I want to spend the rest of my life with," she stressed.

The guide was standing behind the wheel, silently listening to the heated conversation, not volunteering to share what nuggets the Chobe had unearthed that evening.

Beatrice was then miraculously healed from her dumb state. "Your father is not against you marrying whomever you want to marry."

"As long as they are Asian," Tori cut in.

"No, that is not what I was going to say. He does not want you to go through the same stresses we have had to endure all our married life."

It was Tori's turn to be struck with dumbness.

"We had to fight to be together."

"Mmm, it wasn't easy. Remember when we first started to date," Pravin said, shooting his wife an endearing look.

"Yah neh, we were the talk of the school. We had some friends that supported us. Very few, actually. And then we had a large number of haters."

"But we didn't care," Pravin said, getting up from his seat and moving closer to his wife.

Beatrice kissed her husband softly on the back of his hand. "My parents did not have a problem with us dating. It was Pravin's parents that almost toppled over when they found out."

"They threatened me with everything, even cutting me off completely."

"You never told me that," Beatrice said, craning her neck to gaze into her husband's eyes.

"I didn't want to add to all the other things that were happening," he leaned over and kissed his wife's forehead.

"We almost eloped. We thought long and hard about it, but eventually decided to stay and have one traditional wedding that embraced both cultures."

"Did your grandma and grandad attend?" Tori asked.

"Yes, after a lot of conversation with the uncles and the aunties, and, and, and."

"Your dad is the firstborn son, so, for him to marry someone that was not a part of the "clan" was viewed as disrespectful. They viewed it as a great insult."

"I get all that. But you want to tell me, Dad, that you have now adopted your parent's mentality?"

"No, my child, I haven't. I honestly don't care if the chap you end up with is blue, yellow, green, or orange. As long as he loves and respects you, that is all I want. But my apprehension stems from what your mother and I went through."

"And you think I'm too weak to stand up for myself?"

"Well, today you showed us that you have the spine for it. Fight your corner and we will stand by you when the time comes."

Tori got up and walked to her father. "Thank you," she whispered as she gave the man, who smelt of peppermint and beer, a hug.

"So who is he?" Beatrice asked after Tori had sat back down.

"What?"

"The only reason why you would fight for your supposed rights is if there was someone you liked," she said, raising a brow.

"Well," Tori smiled. "I still need to get to know him a little more. But I think he just may be the one," she grinned bashfully.

The Steps

SMALLBOY HAD NOT BEEN TO WORK for a week now. Tori had tried his phone several times but to no avail.

"We have a problem ma'am," It was Lesedi.

"What kind of problem?" Tori enquired.

"Some of our guests have been robbed."

"What!" It was a hollow whisper.

"Mmm."

"What was stolen?"

"A camera, a watch, a phone, some clothes and some pairs of shoes."

"When did this happen?" Tori's mouth had gone dry.

"The day Small boy went missing."

"Heh banna!"

"Mmm," Lesedi made a face.

"Ai! And you haven't seen him anywhere?"

"I haven't, but I heard that he has been going around Kgaphamadi dishing out money, buying his friends shake shake (traditional beer) like he won the lotto."

"Ai," Tori shook her head. "Why haven't the guests come to report?"

"They thought maybe they had misplaced those items, so they

have been backtracking on all the places they have been to. But when they noticed that some of their newly purchased clothes were missing they knew that the theft had happened here at Peter's."

Tori's head was throbbing. She could not make heads or tails of it. Lesedi was the only one that had access to the lofts and here she was, accusing Smallboy of being the culprit. All the evidence pointed to her.

"Thank you for letting me know, I will handle it."

After Tori had finished chatting with her guests, she made her way to the police station. Comfort recognized her and immediately took on her case. That afternoon, Comfort as well as two other officers were at Peter's Place. Tori noticed Lesedi's discomfort when she was being questioned. The officers also questioned Tori's guests. They then took out their equipment and started to dust the areas where the guests had pointed out fingerprints. The back door was crystal clean.

"I cleaned it this morning," Lesedi announced when the policemen pointed out that there were no prints.

Tori looked at her employee suspiciously.

"Maybe the person came through the window," one of the guests suggested.

"Mhm," Comfort bobbed his head and signaled to the man that was dusting for fingerprints to attend to the window.

A few minutes passed as everyone watched the man do his job. The officer then paused at a spot. "Fingerprints!" he announced.

Tori caught Lesedi fidgeting with the cleaning cloth that was in her hand at the corner of her eye.

The men kept dusting for the next hour. After they were satisfied they let Tori know that they would be in touch. Tori apologized to her guests and promised them a fifty percent discount on their stay.

A few days passed. Small boy was still at large. Lesedi's anxiety levels rose.

It was on a Saturday morning when Tori got a call from an unknown number.

"Hello?"

"Ee, Mma Tori?" The man on the other side of the line managed to say her name with a Tswana twang to it.

"Ee rra?"

"Comfortability here," The words were English but the sound, Tswana. "Are you available to come into the office?"

"Yes, I am actually in town, I will be there in five minutes."

"Perfect."

Tori knocked at door number three, ten minutes after the call.

"Come in."

Tori walked in cautiously.

"Good morning?"

"Yes, yes, it is a good morning akere."

"Mhm."

"Ee, so your case mma."

"Ee rra?"

"We managed to find the thief."

Tori's money was on Lesedi, she had already been searching around for a potential candidate to replace her.

"That Smallboy fellow you were telling us about."

"Oh?"

"Yes, yes. It looks like all the items that were stolen, he sold to guys there in Kgaphamadi."

"Uhu!"

"Yes…"

"And where is Smallboy? I have been looking for him all week. He hasn't been to work."

"Well, probably because he was unable to come to work. The boy is at the mortuary."

Tori was flabbergasted, the blood drained from her face, "Mortuary?"

"It happened early this morning actually. We suspect he was on his way back to your lofts to do his job."

"Cleaning?"

"No madam, steal."

"So," Tori shook her head trying to understand. "So what happened to him?"

"Elephant."

Tori tilted her head, "elephant?"

"Mmmm, it looks like the bull got him on the steps."

"Heh banna!" Tori exclaimed in shock.

"Heh banna is correct. So yah, the things he stole are in custody as exhibits at the moment. Once we are able to close the case we will release the items to you."

Tori's brain was still trying to catch up with what Comfort was divulging to her.

"We looked into the boy. It looks like this was his habit," the man pronounced habit, 'habeat'. Each word was Tswanarised with pride and gusto.

"Oh?"

"Yes, he did this back in Mahalapye. We had a case there with him. But there he was going under the alias Tafara. He robbed the people he was working for and disappeared. We have been after him for some time now."

"Wow!" Tori was still digesting the information. Half embarrassed that she had pinned the robberies on the wrong person. She had been ready to sack Lesedi the first moment she got.

"So I just need you to sign these papers and as soon as the case is closed, we will call you in to collect the items that were retrieved."

"Thank you." Tori walked out of the police station still in a daze. She drove up to the Plateau where the steps started to descend, parked on the side, and disembarked. There was a throng at the sight. Police had strung red and white tape around the scene. Journalists were busy at work, like vultures plucking at a corpse. Tori walked up to the red tape. There was nothing to see except blood on the dirt. The elephant was long gone and Smallboy was lying in a vault in a cold room at some random funeral parlor.

As Tori drove into the driveway and parked next to loft three, she caught Lesedi on her way out. It was her half day.

"Sorry Lesedi, I have a bit of bad news."

"I heard."

"Really, wow, news travels fast!"

"Yah, my sister texted me this morning," Lesedi said as she ironed out her dress with her hand out of nerves.

"I wanted to apologise to you."

"Yes?" Lesedi frowned.

"I thought you were the one that had been stealing," Tori confessed, remorse clearly marked on her face.

"I know. I suspected."

"I am so sorry."

"It's okay ma'am. I am the only one that has access to these lofts, I have the keys. It is only logical, I would have suspected me too if I were you."

"Eish, but I feel so bad."

"I was just worried about work. I have young mouths to feed back home, and finding a good-paying job like this one is hard to find. I was really scared I would lose my job."

"Well, you are not losing anything; you are staying right here with me."

The weight on Lesedi's shoulders melted away. Immediately her countenance changed. Her eyes shimmered as tears stung them.

"Now, enjoy the rest of your day and I will see you on Monday bright and early."

"Thank you, ma'am," Lesedi beamed.

That afternoon Tori took a dip in the pool. She was disturbed by a phone call through the landline. Usually when the landline rang it was customers. She dashed out of the pool, and without drying herself dashed to pick up the call.

"Tori speaking, good day."

"Hi, Tsalu?"

"Hey, you."

"Why are you calling my landline?"

"I tried your cell phone several times but you were not picking up."

"Oh, I was in the pool. What's up?"

"Have you picked up a newspaper lately?"

"No, why?"

Mpho huffed on the other end of the call. "Your friend is in the newspaper."

"My friend?" Tori was intrigued.

"Not in a good way," you could hear Mpho flipping through the newspaper.

"Which paper is this, and what friend are you talking about?"

"I actually have Guardian and Mmegi in front of me. Mmegi says and I quote… "The incidents which happened over a period of seven days involved an exchange of fire with armed poachers. The contact areas were Mombo in the Chief's Island, Kurunxaraga, and Selina spillway in the general area of Linyanti.

As succinctly stated previously, there is an alarming surge of rhinoceros poaching in the Okavango Delta and poachers continue to resort to the adoption of ruthless tactics by targeting members of the Botswana Defence Force (BDF). Since the commencement of the year, sixteen armed poachers have been killed.

As a professional, prompt and decisive force, the BDF's anti-poaching units will continue to execute their task of protecting endangered species.

Rhino poaching in Botswana's Okavango Delta has risen at an unprecedented rate with twenty-three white rhinoceros and eight black rhinoceros killed since 2018," the Ministry of Environment, Natural Resources Conservation, and Tourism said.

"This year alone, nine rhinos were killed. The unfortunate incidents have increased with thirteen more rhinos having been poached from January to date," the ministry said in a statement seen by Reuters late on Monday. "Despite heavy rhino poaching in neighbouring South Africa, which has one of the world's largest rhino populations, only six rhinos were killed for their horns in Botswana between two thousand and seven and twenty seventeen," conservation organization Save the Rhino said on its website.

The actual size of the Botswana rhino population is kept a secret by government officials but the Department of Wildlife and National Parks Rhino Coordinator, Dr. Mmadi Reuben, said that if the poaching continued at this rate there will be no rhinos in Botswana in a year or two, especially the black rhino, a critically endangered species.

Botswana is believed to have benefited in the year twenty fifteen when South Africa moved around a hundred rhinos to neighbouring countries as part of efforts to stem the illicit slaughter of the animals for their horns.

Widely regarded as a safe haven for wildlife, Botswana has a strict anti-poaching policy and says it has committed immense resources to combat poaching but poachers have taken advantage of the large size of the Okavango Delta and its difficult wetland terrain. Botswana said it has stepped up efforts to address poaching with interventions leading to the recovery of some horns and hunting weapons.

A rhino horn is estimated by conservationists to be worth more than sixty-five thousand dollars per kilogram with demand rising, particularly in Asia, where a newly affluent class regards it as a status symbol and it is also used as medicine," Mpho finaly ended.

"We should get into this poaching business," Tori said dryly, "did you say sixty-five thousand?"

"Is that all you got from that long read?"Mpho muttered blandly.

"Why do you think one of the poachers is Bastian?"

"His face has been plastered all over the newspaper," Mpho said, obviously exaggerating.

"Are you sure it's him? And why would the papers show pictures of poachers?"

"Why wouldn't they?" Mpho said taking a picture of the image on the newspaper she was holding and sending it to her friend.

Tori squeezed the bone between her eyes and pressed her eyes shut. She felt a young headache tickling the fringes of her brain and then let out a sigh.

"Sorry, Tsalu."

"I was with him just the other day?"

"Yah?"

"Mmm, we bumped into each other ko Cresta Mowana, and enjoyed breakfast together."

"Is it?"

"Yah," Tori's feet were gravitating to the wine rack, she grabbed a wine glass and filled the glass, slightly spilling the wine on the floor. "Ugh!"

"What?"

"I just had a long day, spent it at the police station. There was a robbery here. I think I need to invest in an alarm system."

"You got robbed? When did this happen?"

"The other day, Loft One was broken into and the person stole a couple of things; I had to give the guests a discount. I actually need to send them the police report. They found the thief."

"Oh, that's good. I am shocked actually. That was fast. Kana in Botswana we know there is no rush, so for them to solve your issue that fast is impressive."

"Yah," Tori said as she took a sip from her glass. "I was suspicious of my girl. She is the only one that has access to the lofts."

"Do you think she was working with someone?"

"That was my thought. But it turns out it was my gardener."

"Ai! These people also, you feel sorry for them and you give them the piece jobs they ask for and in return, they spit in your eye."

"Mmm,"

"Sounds like you had a long day."

"I did, the boy is dead."

"Uhu! The police killed him?"

"No, nothing like that. It looks like he was wandering around at night, probably on his way to pull another heist when he came across an angry elephant."

"Eish, kana, those animals can be brutal. Gentle they can be, but under their weight, not so gentle."

"Mmm, am guessing he got in its way or something. They just don't kill for nothing."

"What are you drinking?" Mpho asked.

"Ah, just a cheap red wine, those ones tse di mo specialing."

"Mhm."

"What are you and the family doing today?"

"Mark has taken Bella out for ice cream."

"Mmmk,"

"Yah."

"I had a date with Sebastian kamoso."

"Ahhh…"

"Yah, he wanted to take me on a picnic."

"Sweet."

"Well, looks like I just dodged a bullet," Tori started to laugh.

"What is it?" Mpho joined in the laughter not knowing what the joke was.

"He didn't dodge the bullet."

"Tori, that is not funny."

"I know. I have to laugh. I have had a couple of hectic days."

"At least you had your parents over. How was that?"

"Ah… that was also drama. But at least we finally discussed the whole… dating different races issue."

"How did that go?"

"It went well, actually. I found out that my mom wasn't bothered who I dated, and neither was my dad, it's just that they were afraid I won't be able to handle the flak from relatives."

"Mhm."

"Yah, they told me their story and how they had to fight to be together."

"Oh how sweet!"

"Yah it was nice hearing the story, they have never actually opened up to me about how they met and how they had to stand up to my dad's side of the family."

Mpho was quiet. "Did you finally have the row with them because you wanted to date Sebastian?"

Tori was quiet, she exhaled heavily and finally broke down in tears.

"Aaah tsalu."

"I thought he was the one," Tori said between sobs. "Finally I thought I was going to find happiness."

"Love," Mpho said softly. "No man can give you happiness. Being content is happiness. Never think that happiness is attached to having money, or having a child, or having a man. You are enough. You don't need something tangible to make you happy," Mpho was stern in her delivery.

"You think?"

"I know. I am married and I have a child, but my happiness is not attached to them. I enjoy having them in my life. And they mean the world to me. But they do not define my happiness."

"Thank you for saying that," Tori said, taking a sip of her wine. "I think I have just had a really long day, and the wine is impairing my thinking."

"You are allowed to be emotional. You are allowed to cry. You have carried this burden for years now. You have been in fear of dating because of something that could have been resolved years ago."

"Yah, true. But I think with age, parents are more easily persuaded to accept what we stand up for."

"Yah," Mpho was thoughtful. "Why did you think Sebastian was the one?"

"I didn't think he was the one, I just liked the idea of seeing where things can go if we did try and give it a go."

"You said you thought he was the one, but he was such a slime ball."

"A smooth slime ball," Tori giggled between sips.

"I see you are enjoying that wine."

Tori burst out laughing. "Why aren't you drinking, it's a Saturday, mos."

"Don't worry, as soon as I hang up, I am making myself a cocktail."

"Nice."

"I will check up on you again kamoso neh."

"Sure skeem, thank you for the heads up on Bastian."

"Not a problem."

Elephants Without Borders

THE KGOTLA IN PLATEAU WAS PACKED. The audience, members, the community, the Kgosi, her staff members, police officers, some wildlife personnel, representatives from the clinic, and Lesedi, tucked away at the corner next to her ma'am, Tori. Elephants Without Borders, EWB, a charitable organization, had called a meeting so they could address the community about people's safety around wildlife; a needed presentation after the heinous incident with the elephant that killed Smallboy.

The delegates from the organization sat next to all the other officials upfront. After the Kgosi had addressed those present a man with ginger hair and khaki clothes got up, greeted the crowd warmly, and started off by commending the community for their diligence as well as their willingness to live in harmony with the wildlife in Kasane. "As we all know there is no fence between our town and the national park, so caution is a word we are well familiar with."

Tori and all present sat patiently and attentively as the members from EWB unpacked their presentation on a smart television they had brought along with them. They touched on their EleSenses initiative, bringing to light one of their latest resources in their tool kit, the solar powered electric rope. The electric ropes had already been put in use in certain fields around Kasane.

The solar powered electric rope caught Tori's attention. She made a mental note to install the same sort of fence around her lofts as per Venus' suggestion.

"The EleSenses tools are aimed to be relocatable, adaptable, and easy to use, perfect for a farmer like Dzingani," a peppery man also from EWB was saying, as he clicked a knob on the T.V remote control. An image of a man in his field with a large smile popped up. "We look forward to working with him this year in creating an elephant conflict-free, big harvest."

The audience clapped, impressed by what EWB was achieving in their location.

Another lady was now up, and she presented some scientific findings. "In collaboration with UNSW Science, we have been keeping track of Elephant movements in different human land-uses in Chobe District. I will touch on a few key points. For one, we still have limited understanding of the effects that an increasing human population and urban and agricultural development are having on elephant movements in Botswana. Second, the movements of four female elephants from the Chobe District were studied over a period of 13 months using GPS collars to follow them. These elephant movements were significantly different between different land-use areas, suggesting that elephants could be developing different strategies to move through differing levels of human disturbance. Lastly, it is vital for any wildlife management plan that the spatial movements of key conservation species are thoroughly understood, in order to formulate informed management decisions and create an integrated land-use management plan that enables both development and elephant coexistence," more information on our findings can be found on our website.

Finally an older lady with an American accent got up and talked about the elephant orphanage. A young calf popped on the screen after she pushed a button on the remote. "This is Boipuso; she was rescued due to a tragic incident that took place, where she was intercepted at a local tavern and harassed by patrons of the bar. At only 2 months old, she was confused, lost and no one knew the whereabouts of her mother or family herd. She had several bruises and cuts, but after two months of intensive care, she fully accepted the team and has become the center of everyone's attention, including the calf herd. She is very clever, learning quickly from the other elephants. We are very pleased to see her grow and develop. Her weight has doubled in six months under our care!"

The woman clicked the remote and another calf popped up. "Panda was discovered alone in a farmer's fenced field in Pandamatenga, in Chobe, a northern District of Botswana. Despite waiting several days in hopes of being able to reunite her with her herd, no other elephants were seen or heard from. After fending off a pack of hyenas, the farmer concluded Panda had little chance of survival on her own, and contacted us to care for her. Since then, Panda has grown to become the young matriarch of the elephants residing at the orphanage, settling in and tending to all the younger elephants." The lady clicked the remote again, "lastly we have Tuli, she is only a month old, tiny Tuli came from the Tuli Block, the mid-east portion of Botswana. After an unfortunate human-conflict situation, Tuli lost her family and was found wandering by a lodge owner. She was airlifted by EWB's rescue plane and arrived on-site that same day of call-in. Tuli was in critical care but is now integrated into the small herd and full of spunk! She has bonded tightly with Panda and follows her adopted big sister everywhere."

The lady then directed her attention to the community. "It is said it takes a village to raise a child. This is also true of elephants. We need your help to care for these little Ellies. You may wonder what you could do to assist. Elephants Without Borders heavily relies on donations, funds, and grants to keep afloat. Each donation is vital to our mission, so we urge those that can to please make a donation to our cause."

After the presentation was over Tori stealthily made her way to the American lady that had made her presentation on the orphanage. "Sorry, she said shyly. I was captivated by your presentation. I would love to do something if possible to help."

"Yah?"

"Please. One of my staff members was trampled by an elephant recently, which is why I am here actually. Sort of like a team-building thing. But I wouldn't mind actually taking this further for my girl," Tori said, pointing at Lesedi. She has young children, and would love, if possible, to take them on a day trip at your orphanage, if this is something you do."

"Yes, we would love to have you over. How does tomorrow sound?"

"Sounds perfect actually. I am looking forward to it. And when I am there, please let me know where I can make a donation."

"You know what is best. Just go on our website, under donate, just follow the instructions there. It's pretty easy."

"Thank you," Tori said, proud she had approached the EWB staff member. "See you tomorrow then."

"Sure."

Gerald and Venus

THE DOG HAD A LOUD BARK FOR IT'S SIZE.

"Stop it," Venus reprimanded.

The little poodle kept barking something wicked. The bark got louder and louder the closer Tori approached.

"I said stop it!" Venus shouted, "You are being naughty. She is our friend." Venus walked to the gate and let Tori in. "How are you, my dear?" Venus greeted between barks.

"I am well, thank you."

The poodle was at Tori's heels trying to bite her ankles.

Venus slightly nudged the dog with her foot. "You hooligan! Pixie, stop it now, shut up! Shut up! The barking drives me mad!" Venus' tone changed. She gave the fluffy dog a long stern glare.

Pixie whined a little and let out a few barks at Venus.

"Don't you dare talk back to me? I will shapa you!" The poodle quickly ran into the house after hearing the word shapa.

Venus smiled at Tori, "Come, come," she ushered Tori into the house.

Tori cautiously followed. The house was crammed full of antiques, trinkets, and wooden furniture. Pixie had retreated under one of the wooden chairs, pouting as she watched Tori at a distance.

Venus smiled at her guest. "Take a seat hon. Let me bring the ice tea." She hobbled to the kitchen, prepared three glasses, filled them with ice then poured the cool beverage topping all three glasses.

Venus smiled as she handed Tori a glass. "It's ice tea, I don't put too much sugar in it, when I do I find I drink a lot of water after having it. So I hold off on the sugar a bit. It's very refreshing," she smiled proudly. "Let me know if you would like a refill."

Tori nodded as she took a sip from the beverage. "It was basically cold weak tea, with a touch of sugar. She plastered a fake smile and nodded, "refreshing," was the word that came out of her mouth, afraid if she really said how the drink was it would bruise Venus' ego.

"Let me take my Gerald his juice, he is in his nursery. I'll be back just now dearest."

After Venus left Tori took a moment to look at the family pictures that were on the wall. There were many pictures of who Tori assumed was Gerald in the bush with a tribe of bushmen.

"Oh," Tori heard Venus as she walked through the front door. "Those are pictures of our Gerald. He would like to come and say hi, but he is preoccupied at the moment."

"Has he always been into gardening, your Gerald?" Tori asked as she continued gazing at the pictures on the wall.

"It developed over the years. He was into animals. He worked for the department of wildlife for a while, till they wrongfully sullied his name. When we had the farm, he got into growing more things."

Tori paused at a picture. "Are those twins?"

A shadow cast over Venus. "Yes, James and John, sons of thunder," Venus' voice had a melancholy ring to it. "We had three children, my Gerald and I. John, James, and Peter."

"Where are they now," Tori asked quietly.

"Dead," she said, before turning away.

"Oh, dear." Tori was sorry she asked.

"Yah. James and John did not reach their sixth birthday.

Meningitis."

"Oh, shame. I am so sorry Venus."

"Yah, it was a long time ago."

Tori was now afraid to ask about Peter.

"Peter was twenty when he died," Venus' face went dark.

Tori was silent, she backed away from the wall that was bringing back sore memories to Venus and took a seat on the rocking chair that had Scandinavian colours.

Venus followed suit, resting on her two seater antique chair. "It was a buffalo. He was walking home one day, poor lad, minding his own business. He used The Steps and there was a lone buffalo hanging about. The Cape buffalo is a formidable creature. It earned the name 'black death' because of its wicked reputation. A lone buffalo is actually regarded as one of the most dangerous wildlife. We got a call from the police, asking us to come to The Steps and identify our boy. Just like that. No sorry for what happened. No sympathy. No human feeling. Just a metallic voice over the phone. When we got there, it was our Peter. His lifeless body on display for all to see, it was the worst day of my life! My Gerald took it really badly. He used to be outgoing and loved spending time in the bush. But when that buffalo killed our Peter, he barricaded himself in his little lab slash nursery. I hardly see him. We hardly talk."

Tori was in shock, she couldn't imagine the amount of pain Venus and Gerald had gone through, losing three sons, three heirs. It was just terrible. "I am so sorry Venus."

Venus shook her head. "It's not your fault. That demonic animal is to blame."

There was a pregnant silence. Tori took another sip from her bland ice tea to distract herself.

"Anyway, sorry for telling you that story. It dampens the merriment. We are meant to be having a good time," Venus tried to smile.

"I know, I am sorry I asked."

"The pictures are on display. It is only natural for you to ask."

Pixie made an appearance from under the chair. She cautiously walked to where Tori was sitting, and brushed herself on Tori's foot.

"She is looking for attention," Venus smiled.

"She is really pretty."

"Yah, she was a gift. Gerald left to go to town one day, and came back with her. He says he rescued her or something."

"Oh how sweet," Tori said as she rubbed Pixie.

What both ladies didn't know was that Gerald had stolen Pixie. She had been wandering outside her owner's yard in Lesoma, and Gerald happened to be passing by on his way from helping a silly woman who had allowed herself to be cornered by a snake. Gerald immediately took it upon himself to "rescue" Pixie and told his wife the dog was a gift.

"Are you thinking of getting a dog, Tori? They are good company."

"Well, with living at Peter's Place, I don't think I would get a dog. Unless it was one that doesn't bark," she giggled. "A dog would make too much noise for my guests. If I move, or should I say, when I move, then I will think of getting a dog."

Venus shook her head. "Are you thinking of moving?"

"Yes," Tori said, glancing at Venus for a second before continuing to stroke Pixie.

"Why, that place is so homely!"

"Well, I am thinking of making loft three available for tourists. I get a lot of them knocking at my door at odd hours to assist with this and that. If I am not on the premises then it will make my life a little less stressful," She smiled.

"Well if you ever think of getting a dog don't take them to the vet on President Avenue. One time Mrs. Smith down the road took her little Shih Tzu's to that vet for a rabies shot, by the time they were out of the gate all her puppies were dead. So, I am not sure about that vet down that road. I don't know if he was using old medicinal techniques, or he just didn't know what he was doing. If you think of getting a little puppy, just bring it here and our Gerald can take care of them for you. He gives Pixie her vaccinations, he is the one that fixed her too. I trust my Gerald, and he won't charge you." Venus smiled.

Tori obliged.

"Would you like some ice cream?"

"I would love some," Tori beamed.

"I know I was supposed to cook. But I got lazy, which is why I am offering you everything else but solid food," she giggled as she wobbled to the kitchen.

"No, that's fine," Tori smiled sheepishly. "Ice cream sounds perfect."

Venus reappeared from the kitchen with two bowls of ice cream. "There you go," she said as she brushed her hair. "I have been thinking of going to get my haircut at the salon. I am afraid to go. I have never been there. My Gerald always cuts my hair. But he always cuts it too short," Venus complained between scoops of ice cream. "I told him I am a big girl and not to cut it so short because after he has cut it I always look like a coconut bobbing on the sea," she chuckled, "see here," she turned to show the back of her head, "it is thinning," using her left hand, she flicked her back hair.

Tori smiled. "It looks fine to me."

"What do you know," Venus smiled. "You have long luscious hair."

Tori only shook her head as she enjoyed her ice cream.

"You know at night, we get bush babies,"

"Wow, really?"

"Yes, you don't get any at the lofts?"

"Well, I haven't seen any…"

"It might be because of all the lights you have there. But my Gerald and I get bush babies here. They jump on the roof. Pixie goes mad with the slightest sound. She drives me mad with the barking. But they are the cutest things," Venus said, stressing the word cutest.

Tori chuckled.

"So my girl, what is your story? I told you all about my boys. What about your family? Do you have any siblings?"

"Yes actually. I have two older brothers. They live abroad, both married."

"And why haven't you found someone yet?"

"He ended up being a poacher."

"Oh, my giddy aunt!" Venus gasped.

"Yah… We were not dating, but we were supposed to go out on a date. The day before the date, I found out he was shot dead by the anti-poaching team."

"Well, I must say you dodged a bullet there, dear. You have to be careful when it comes to dating. It's a tricky business finding the right match."

"How did you and Gerald meet? How did you know you were the right match?"

"On Blue Jacket Street actually, I was struggling with the groceries I had bought, and he came to my rescue. We were good friends to start with and the friendship grew into romance, and the rest is history."

"Mmhm."

"That is the best way you know, getting to know someone as a friend first before you rush into other 'stuff'. You get to know what ticks them off, how they react when they are ticked off. How they treat others, if they are a nasty piece of work or are genuine. You get to know a lot about a person when romance is not attached. The person gets to be themselves and you get to watch from a distance before your heart gets too attached."

"Yah, well I thought I knew this guy."

"Who, the poacher? No dear, your emotions were attached before you knew the person in and out."

Tori breathed heavily, "I guess, my best friend tried to warn me but I didn't listen."

"Red flag babe, never ignore the red flags. If someone is telling you there is something wrong, don't take it so personally. Ask yourself what they see that you don't. Most times when our emotions are attached we brush off things that would normally niggle us. And once you ignore one thing, you will give concessions to many things. Never compromise!"

"You think so?" Tori asked with a frown on her head.

"Can you imagine living with a poacher in the house? That means you will have dead animal heads hung around your house. Do you want that? It will mean guns. Do you want those in your home? What if one day you have an argument and you end up being his target? Poachers are angry people. They have no sense. And they kill these poor animals for what?" Venus asked rhetorically. "To sell in the black market to some Asian hoodlum that would like to use it for "medicinal purposes"" she said, making quotes in the air. "These people are dirty and greedy. I would never trust a poacher hon. NEVER!" she stressed.

Tori blinked. "Mpho, the friend I was telling you about, she said there was something unbecoming about him."

"And you didn't believe her?"

"Well, I knew the guy when we were in high school."

"Before you started dating him, how long was it since you saw him?"

"Well, we were not dating. The last time I saw him actually was when I completed my form five, so probably more than ten years ago."

"So, the boy you knew way back then, is not the man he was now."

"Mmm, I guess you are right."

"I know I am right."

"Then there is this other guy that I really like. But I don't know. I think maybe we are not a good match."

"What makes you say that?"

"Well, I haven't spent that much time with him to know."

"So why would you jump to the conclusion that you were a bad match."

"I don't know."

Venus tilted her head, "You are not telling me everything."

"Well. I kinda pushed him away."

Venus let out a little laugh. "You pushed him away for the poacher!" her laughter kept catching fire and got louder and louder.

"Well, it's not that funny," Tori said, getting a little upset.

Venus coughed between giggles, "I am sorry dear," she put on a serious face, "yes, the other guy. Tell me about him."

"Well, there is really nothing to tell. We have spent a bit of time together. I know his background, and my best friend seems to like him and vouches for him."

"Well honey, my money is on your best friend. She seems to

know how to tell what's fake from what is real."

"I guess, she has a wonderful marriage and a gorgeous daughter."

"Is that what you want, children?" Venus' voice saddened slightly.

"Erm, not really, no, actually, I don't think I want them. I love children. I just think they are not for me."

"But you would like someone to spend the rest of your life with?"

"Yes, exactly!" Tori said shyly.

"Does this mystery man feel the same?"

"I don't know?"

"These are things you need to establish. As I mentioned, getting to know the person is paramount. The main reason why marriages don't work is that you are both in the same house but are on two different paths. He may want children. If you don't want them that may be a deal-breaker."

"Really?" Tori was shocked that having or not having children was an issue that could lead to separation or possibly a divorce.

"Yep, many marriages don't work because of things like that. What about his work habits? Does he actually have a job? You don't want someone dragging you down. You seem like a strong independent woman, be careful not to end up with someone as strong as you, or weaker. They need to be stronger. And I am not talking about money. You are a go-getter. Is he the same? Does he push you to do better, or are you the one that is always doing the pushing? You need to find balance."

"But aren't these the things I will get to know when we are dating?"

"No," Venus shook her head. "These are things you can see and learn from a safe distance."

"I have never really had a male friend."

"I suggest you always meet this person in groups, not just the two of you, that way you are able to watch the person without the pressure of trying to impress."

Tori nodded, her smile gone awry.

Venus suddenly jumped up. "Agh I hate spiders!" she screeched. "Pass me that feather duster that looks like a molding ostrich dear," she pointed.

Tori followed Venus' gaze.

"Yes, that one on the table, this place is just full of gogos you would think the foundation was made from them."

Tori obediently handed the old woman the feather duster and watched as Venus used it to swat the spider that was on her chair.

"More ice cream?" Venus offered, looking at Tori's empty bowl.

"No, no. I've had enough. In fact, I should be getting home."

"Ahhh, shame, I thought my Gerald would have made an appearance, so you can meet him."

"Maybe next time," Tori said, giving Venus an endearing smile. "I have really enjoyed my afternoon with you."

Venus got up. "Let me walk you to your car."

As soon as Tori got up Pixie turned on her and started barking at her again.

"Pixie you are rude!" Venus roared. "This is our guest's mxm! Come come, Tori, let's lock this one up in the house," she said, pushing Tori out the door with her wrinkled hand while pushing Pixie back in the house with her pasty leg that resembled a crow's foot.

As the pair walked out, Venus found yet another thing to moan about. "Her poop is all over and it makes me sick. I need to put a cork in Pixie's bum," she said, shaking her head, causing Tori to burst out laughing.

Once they reached the outskirts of the tree and shrub clustered yard to Tori's Surf, Tori couldn't help but smile at her new found friend and aunt as she gave her a squeeze and kissed her softly on the cheek.

"Thank you for popping by, honey, and I promise next time there will be a meal on the table for you," Venus uttered into Tori's ear before she let her go.

"No worries Aunt Venus, I really appreciate the company."

"What I can't understand is why you want to be hanging around an old geezer like me. Go out there and find yourself some real friends," she said, flicking her hand as though to tell Tori to soka.

"You are my real friend," Tori smirked.

Bush Babies

EVER SINCE TORI FOUND OUT that there were bush babies about, she made it her sole purpose to try and find them. The problem was that her place was flooded with light.

"Dusk," Aunt Venus had said, "I can see them at dusk," she looked at her watch, and then peeked outside; the sun was still prominently dominating the sky. "In an hour I guess," Tori whispered.

She walked to the couch, threw herself on it, reached for the television remote, and turned to the news channel. It had been a while since she had caught up with all the terrible things that were happening across the globe. A lady dressed in a blue Egyptian dress was on the screen, highlighted in red was a bold headline that read -Wuhan Coronavirus- below, in a grey box, Tori read the bold type words, "Official: nine dead, at least 470 infected in China." Tori increased the volume, walked to her little kitchen to pour herself a glass of wine, and pop some corn. The woman on the screen was speaking…

"Sars-like virus, which has infected hundreds in China, has now reached the United States. Airports around the world are stepping up health screening of passengers arriving from Wuhan China, the epicenter of the outbreak. Nine people have died in China, and at least 470 are infected, there are fears that corona virus will spread during the busy Lunar New Year period. Besides the US, cases have already been reported in South Korea, Japan and in Thailand." The screen was showing a map of the world with all the countries that had been infected with the virus highlighted in red. Tori pressed the pause button; the sound of the popping corn was overpowering the news presenter. Once the popping died down a bit, she pressed play. "The virus was first identified at a market in the city of Wuhan last month, which sells seafood and live animals."

Tori looked for a container to pour her freshly made popcorn, seasoned it with Aromat, threw a few fluffy popcorns in her mouth, and smiled. She took a long sniff of the wine she had bought and proceeded to take a long sip. She rejoined the woman on the screen who was now chatting with a man that seemed to be based in China.

"David, talk to us from what you have seen as to how the Chinese government announced stepping up their response to this as the Lunar New Year is beginning."

There was a little pause, then David, who was on the screen side by side with the lady in blue with a heavy American accent, started to speak.

"The biggest concern, Christiana, is the time of year. This is when there is the largest human migration each year; you've got millions of people travelling. We were among them in the crowd, we took the train from Beijing to Wuhan last night and we were able to get the feeling of just how closely people travel together. So that is the greatest concern, this is actually the first time we have been able to take off our face masks but I keep it close to me. We are on an elevated level, a balcony, secluded away from the crowds, but as soon as we get to the streets, we and most people here put the mask back on. This is our opportunity to bring you to what is the epicenter of this illness," the man then went mute and the screen changed the scene to the streets of what Tori assumed was Wuhan. There was a lone man walking on a deserted street, Chinese writing on a blue tape surrounding a barricaded area, another voice was now booming through the screen.

"This is ground zero for the illness setting global unease."

The man who had been side by side on the screen with

Christiana was back on the screen, this time with a mask on. "So this is where officials believe the source of the coronavirus is," the camera angle shifted, showing the man pointing at a building in the distance. Tori took a sip of her wine as she continued to munch on her popcorn. "The wildlife and seafood market, and you can see it's been cordoned off, you've got police at all corners.

"It is so sensitive that within minutes of us arriving and recording, security asked us to stop filming. There is an uneasiness felt throughout Wuhan. We experienced that as soon as we boarded the train from Beijing. Each cart was nearly full, most spaces covered. Just about everyone travelling home for the Lunar New Year, strict screening upon arrival, one by one, passengers stepped through a thermometer check, to make sure they are not bringing the fever with them. Scenes like these are playing out in transportation hubs throughout China."

Tori shook her head; she reached for her phone to call Mpho.

"Have you seen the news?"

"Mark and I are watching it now."

"Mathata," Tori was shaking her head as she watched the screen.

"Mmm, but it's in China, it won't get here," Mpho said casually.

"This thing is already in America. It will soon hit Africa.

"Mark says he thinks it's some virus cooked in a lab."

Tori laughed. "What makes him think that?"

"Ah. There are many conspiracy theories flying around at the moment."

"Well let's hope it doesn't come to Botswana, otherwise we are doomed!"

"It will shut down businesses," Tori heard Mark say.

"Mmm, it's going to crash a lot of businesses, including mine." Eish, can you imagine what will happen if tourists stop coming to

Botswana, it will bring the tourism industry down to its knees."

"We will recover," Tori realized Mpho had put her on loudspeaker. Mark was dominating the conversation.

"After a while, yes we will recover but we will be crippled."

"Remember the Spanish Flu. It also swept through the globe, but eventually, we recovered. So just like this virus as long as we are forewarned, we will be forearmed. The Government needs to act fast."

"I think we should start stocking up on food. If Masisi shuts down the borders, where are we going to get supplies from?" Tori's mind was racing; she gulped down the rest of the wine in her glass and walked over the wine rack for a refill.

"Yah, we need to start thinking about little survival bunkers. If things go bad, we may need to stay in our homes for some time to try and contain the situation."

"Mark, you really think Botswana will get to that?" Tori heard Mpho ask.

"I wouldn't put it past the governments to try that strategy, slowing down the spread."

"Mmm, sounds hectic. Think I need to go to the store tomorrow and stock up. Ai, it just messes up everything. I was hoping to start working on my place."

"Your plans were approved?"

"Not yet, but any day now," Tori huffed.

"Well hang on tight; you may need that money to tie you over should there be a crash in the economy.

"Mmm, you are right." Tori was thoughtful. "Yah, let's see how things play out. I got to go guys, I am in search of bushbabies tonight."

"In the bush?" Mpho asked.

"Yah, but I will be sitting in my backyard; I am going to turn off all the lights. They say you are able to see them at dusk. And by they, I mean Aunt Venus," Tori smiled to the phone, "so I'm going to grab a chair and go sit in the yard hunting for bush babies."

"Wish I were there with you," Mpho said.

"I have an extra chair out back waiting for you," Tori teased.

"Enjoy your evening Tori," Mark said with a smile in his voice.

"Thanks, Mark."

"How is Bella?"

"She is sleeping, they keep them busy at school, so by the time she gets home, she is completely tired."

"Well, let me go search for my bush babies, otherwise I will miss them."

"Cool, chat to you soon."

"Night night."

Carnage

THE TOURISTS AT PETER'S PLACE were slowly becoming long term tenants. Tori's lofts were being booked by Peace Corp as well as specialists that were part of an NGO based in Kazungula, called Acacia. To accommodate her long term residents, Tori decided to adjust the prices to better suit lengthy stays.

A car pulled in the driveway with an Acacia sticker on its side. A woman dressed in khakis jumped out of the passenger side and proceeded to remove her luggage from the back of the bakkie.

"Good afternoon," Tori approached her guest with a welcoming smile.

The woman swung around to face Tori, "Good afternoon," she said, returning the smile, "My name is Billie-Jean, BJ for short," the woman stretched out her hand to greet Tori.

Tori gave the tan Californian native a good handshake. The woman had long dark hair with natural silver highlights. She looked prim and proper to Tori, not someone bent on roughing it in the bush for six months. But then again maybe the book was hardier than it seemed, Tori thought to herself. "Acacia?"

"Yes, correct."

"I am Tori."

"Wonderful!"

"You are staying for six months, correct?" Tori said, consulting her tablet.

"Correct."

"Okay, you will be in Loft one. This way please." Tori said ushering the woman to the first loft on the property.

"This is beautiful," Billie-Jean said.

Tori smiled, "Thank you. So let me just show you around. This is the lounge," she started stating the obvious. "And over here we have the kitchenette." Tori pointed at the island prep station that housed a microwave drawer and a farmhouse-style double basin sink.

Billie-Jean walked over to have a look, she flung open the drawers, and cupboards, a smile glued on her face as she was greeted by matching coffee mugs, cutlery, fresh towels, a percolator, an electric kettle, a modest fridge, and a house fern that spruced up the little galley. "This is really neat. I love it."

Tori beamed, "Over here you have your backyard, with your own private pool." Tori opened the floor-to-ceiling - curtains to expose the backyard. She slid the glass doors open, letting Billie-Jean take in the simple yet sophisticated beauty she had spent months working on.

For a moment she thought of that ungrateful man, Small Boy, who got trampled on by a hormonal elephant on The Steps.

It was on a Sunday afternoon that Billie-Jean came knocking at Tori's door.

"Sorry to disturb you."

Tori tilted her head slightly, "Is everything okay?"

"No, actually, I have been waiting all morning for the guys at our camp to come and pick me up. There has been an incident that I need to attend to. But all of our cars are out."

Tori quickly surmised what Billie-Jean was getting at. "Do you need me to drop you somewhere?"

"Please," BJ's face pleaded. "Our base is in Kazungula."

"Okay, let me change quickly and I will be with you in a sec."

Twenty minutes later, the ladies drove into the site. It was quiet. BJ spotted a handful of workers feeding a few elephants. She jumped out of the car and headed for the man that was pulling a hosepipe. Tori stayed in the car and watched from a distance. This was all new to her. She didn't even know that a place like this existed.

"Hey KB," she heard BJ say.

"Hi," the man responded.

"I heard about the buffalo!"

"Yes, most of the guys left this morning to go and check out what happened."

"Do you know where they are?"

"Erm, no," Tori heard KB say, "But I guess you can pick up the walkie-talkie and try and catch them where they are."

Tori watched as KB and BJ walked into what she assumed to be the office. A few minutes later, she spotted BJ, rushing to the back of the building, only to re-appear with a gun in hand.

As Billie –Jean hopped back into the car, Tori couldn't help but stare at the weapon BJ had in her hand.

Noticing her host's look, BJ smiled, "Oh, it's a dart gun. I have the tranquillizer here," she said, producing three darts.

"Mmm, so what is happening?" Tori quizzed, as she shook her head.

"There has been a sighting of a herd of buffalo in the Chobe."

"Yah?"

"They are all dead."

Tori felt as though she was experiencing déjà vu. "Dead Buffalo?"

"Yah."

"This sounds like the same thing that happened about two years ago."

"Yah?"

"Mmm, there was a herd of elephants that were affected as well as a herd of buffalo. Nobody really knows the real cause of the animals' deaths, some people speculated that it was Tsetse Fly."

"Mmm, from the looks of this, we don't think it is the Tsetse fly. The guys have been at the site since morning," BJ paused awkwardly.

Tori gazed at her quickly before focusing on the road again. "What aren't you saying BJ?"

"It looks like hundreds of buffalo Tori, thousands maybe."

Tori was in shock.

"Yah, so we need to find out what is going on."

"Do you know exactly where your crew is?"

"I am going to try and track them down with the walkie. I tried their cellphones, but the reception is bad. So the walkie' is all we have."

"Okay," Tori stepped on the accelerator.

When they reached the outskirts of the park, BDF was there, boots strapped in, guns in hand, determined looks on their faces. BJ walked into the little office, before quickly darting out and giving Tori the nod to follow one of the green military jeeps in front of them. The jeep sped carefully through the park leading to the buffalo massacre. There was carcass after carcass. Vultures stared longingly at the carnage from the tree tops while lions, cheetahs, and hyena's gawked on from a distance. There was something disturbing about the scene. To Tori, this should have been a predator's dream; however, it seemed to her that all the hunters from the animal kingdom were cautious onlookers.

"What killed all these buffalo?" Tori gasped.

"Exactly!" All the blood in BJ's face had drained. Her lips chapped, and her hands were shaky. "This is not normal," she whispered as she carefully disembarked after the Toyota Surf had come to a halt.

Tori watched in horror. BJ had spotted one of her colleagues and was walking towards him. The man was shaking his head. There was something about him that looked familiar but Tori couldn't really place him. She watched as BJ pointed towards her, the man's eyes followed BJ's finger and found herself looking straight into the man's eyes.

"Glen?" Tori whispered. She had not clapped eyes on the man for more than two years. The last she had seen him was in Kasane after the first Buffalo case they had encountered. She watched as Glen marched her way. Tori unbuckled before sliding out of the driver's seat. "Glen," she smiled, "What are you doing here?"

Glen smiled warmly back, before gesturing to the carnage. "We heard about it late last night. One of the guides had taken some campers on a night drive, and came across this. I flew in this morning."

"This is not the Tsetse fly, is it?" Tori asked.

Glen shook his head, "No. It looks like Rinderpest, I need to take the samples I collected to a lab to confirm."

Tori looked at Glen blankly.

"The last confirmed case was in two thousand and one," Glen said as he leaned on Tori's car. "The disease affects animals with hooves. Buffalo, antelope, deer, giraffe, warthogs, even our cattle."

"That sounds scary."

"It is. It could potentially wipe out thousands and thousands of domestic animals as well as the wildlife here. If we don't do something quickly, we will have a serious problem."

Tori was silent for a few minutes. She gazed at the scene laid out in front of them.

"The BDF have been summoned to help keep predators at bay. Up until we can confirm what killed these buffalo, so we are trying to contain this area."

"Mhm," Tori noticed how the National Defense Force had encircled the deceased buffalo. The men in camouflage garb were armed and fully alert."

"What are you going to do?"

"The only thing we can do is burn the buffalo here, after collecting samples. After which we will need to spray the area just to make sure."

"Mmm," Tori said passively.

"What are you thinking?"

"You say that the disease affects other species as well."

"Well yes."

"So how come all the other animals are fine?"

"What do you mean?"

"I mean, do you see any antelope, warthogs, and giraffes amongst the carnage?"

"Well, no. But…"

"So if it is this Rind disease you are telling me about, why would it be selective?" Tori said, thinking out loud.

"Well," Glen huffed. "That is what we are planning to find out."

Tori nodded, as her nose reacted to the wafts of decaying game being gently carried through the atmosphere by a soft breeze.

"Do you have any vacancies?"

"Vacancies?"

"Yes, at your lofts?"

"Oh, no, sorry, they are all occupied," Tori apologized.

"Seems as though everything is fully booked," Glen said, adjusting his cap.

"Yah?"

"Mmm, but I'll sort something out."

"Are you sure?"

"Yah,"

Tori looked at the man, knowing full well he was not going to find accommodation. "I tell you what, why don't you come and stay at my place. It's actually one of the lofts; I will sort something out for myself."

"Are you sure about that?"

"Yes, I have a good friend that I hope will accommodate me for a few days, or weeks, if you plan to stay longer."

"Tori, are you absolutely sure?" Glen's eyes were shining with hope.

"Yes, I am very sure."

"Thank you so much. I was going to sleep at the camp in the car or in the office."

Tori laughed aloud, "I thought as much. There is plenty of room, in case you have any colleagues you came with?"

"No, it's just me actually. Mark sent me as soon as we heard."

"Is that how you found out about my lofts?"

"Yes, he suggested that I stay there. So you can send the bill to the office?"

"Sure, I will be sure to charge you extra for hijacking my place," Tori teased.

Venus was delighted to have Tori stay with her for two weeks.

"My Gerald will not notice you are even here. He has been staying in that wretched nursery of his for weeks on end. He doesn't shower, he doesn't eat, he is just obsessed with that place."

"Thank you for having me, Aunt Venus."

Pixie had been in her usual form, barking up a storm the minute she saw Tori walk in with her bags.

"This will be your room," Venus announced.

Tori nodded as she took in all the clutter. "I am sure I will be cozy," she smiled sheepishly.

"So you say you let out your loft?"

"Yes, there has been an influx of visitors in Kasane, and places are fully booked."

"You did mention you wanted to have the third loft let out."

"Yes, but I had put that on hold due to this pandemic that seems to be coming our way. Have you heard that it is now in South Africa? Apparently, eight people are infected."

"They just need to shut down the borders," Venus said, "No one in, no one out."

"Then what are we going to do for food?" Tori chuckled.

"I would suggest you start stocking up on food. I have always said that Botswana relies too much on its neighboring countries for food. We need to start being self-sufficient," Venus said as she laid out some fresh towels for Tori.

"True, I guess," Tori smiled.

"So there is no air con in this room. What I can do at night is leave my door open, so you can feel the air- conditioner from my room. We share the bathroom and toilet. The kitchen is here. Feel free to help yourself."

"Thanks, Aunt Venus," Tori said as she slipped an envelope into the old woman's hand.

"What is this now?"

"My way of thanking you."

Venus opened the envelope and was confronted by wads of cash. "I can't accept this," she said, pushing the envelope back into Tori's hands.

"Yes, yes you can. I will be using your water, your electricity, eating your food. The least I can do is thank you. And besides, I am making money by staying here. If it weren't for you I wouldn't have been able to lease out loft three."

Venus was thoughtful. "Okay, fine, if you put it that way, I accept," the old woman said, snatching back the envelope.

The act was so abrupt it put a grin on Tori's face.

That evening it rained heavily, causing Venus' house to be stuffier than before. The smell of Pixie permeated the house. When Tori tried to open the windows she was confronted by the smell of Pixie's poo in the back yard. After popping her head out to see why the smell was so potent, she realized that Venus had been using the back yard as her dumping spot for Pixie's poop.

"My Days!" she whispered as she felt her nose block.

Cape Buffalo

IT HAD BEEN A MONTH SINCE THE HORRENDOUS incident with the Cape Buffalo. Specialists had flown in from all parts of the world to lend a hand in trying to figure out the mind-boggling mystery. Glen mentioned to Tori that indeed the disease was Rinderpest. But what was bizarre was that the virus seemed to just target the Cape Buffalo, as though it had been designed specifically for the Syncerus caffer caffer.

Tori found herself visiting the Acacia camp more and more often. There was something about BJ. Maybe it was the woman's unpretentious attitude, or her bonny smile, or her little laugh, or her glorious caramel skin. Or maybe it was her name. Tori admitted that she had never heard of anyone named Billie-Jean.

The friends spent afternoons together at the Acacia camp. Tori's knowledge of wild animals was vastly enriched. There were close to thirty staff members, a majority being Batswana. There was an elephant orphanage, where close to fifteen caretakers spent hours in the day caring for motherless calves. This was where Tori loved to hang out. She had made a connection with a little calf named Willow. The nine month-old, little gray giant lost its mother to poachers. She wondered if the reason why she was so drawn to the baby was because she had almost dated a poacher and in a funny way felt responsible for the little Ellis' mother's demise. She was feeding the baby one afternoon while patting the baby's little nappy head when Glen approached.

"They are the sweetest aren't they?"

Tori was a little startled to see Glen at the camp. "Yes, yes they are," she said as she tried to ignore the butterflies in her stomach. She leaned over to kiss the calf, to disguise her nerves before turning back to Glen, shooting him a gaze that lodged a quizzical brow. "What brings you here?"

"Oh, I came to see BJ."

"Oh?" Tori felt a tinge of jealousy flush on her face.

"Yah, we have been working on the Rinderpest case."

"Yah?"

"Yah, it seems like the thing is homemade."

The shock on Tori's face was apparent.

"Yah, don't say anything to anyone."

"Can people do that?"

"Yes, it is not easy, but for someone who studied virology or similar subjects, and had a lab with all the right equipment, it is very possible to concoct something, all you need is the virus itself and a living organism to multiply it."

"Why do you think it's home brewed?"

"It's what you mentioned that time at the siting. That all the other animals that should be affected were not affected. We monitored that, and found that indeed the virus was tailor-made for just the Cape buffalo."

"But why? That doesn't make any sense."

"That is what we are trying to figure out."

"Oh!"

"So have you seen her?"

"Who?

"BJ."

"No, sorry, I saw her when coming in, she was at the office, but I've been with this little one for close to thirty minutes now, she could be anywhere."

"Oh," he huffed. "Let me try her cellphone then."

Tori found that the little green monster inside of her was growing even more. She hadn't thought Glen and BJ would get on the way they were. She practically pushed the man away years back, and when she finally saw him again, pushed him into the arms of an African American goddess. "Mxm."

"What was that?"

Tori didn't realize that Glen was still standing next to her.

"Oh, nothing I was just thinking of the poachers that took away Willow's mother," she lied.

"Mmm, a shame isn't it?"

"A very big shame!" she said, avoiding Glen's eyes.

"She isn't answering her phone. Do you mind telling her I was looking for her?"

"Sure, no problem," Tori said, producing a halfhearted smile.

"See you around," Glen said, nudging Tori's shoulder.

That evening when Tori got back to her temporary abode, she found Venus in the garden.

"What are you up to?" she smiled.

"Oh, my Gerald just asked if I could remove the weeds."

Tori looked at the woman as she was on her knees busy de-weeding the grass. She plunked her bag on a nearby chair and knelt down near Venus. "Why don't you get a gardener?"

"Oh, my Gerald says we don't need a gardener. He says he is capable of taking care of the garden himself. But the problem is, he barricades himself in the little nursery all day and neglects all other things and I end up being the one that does the yard work," she giggled dryly.

Tori was failing to understand the dynamics of Aunt Venus and Gerald's relationship. It was pretty bizarre. The more she tried to comprehend, the more perplexed she was.

"We are having baked potatoes and cheesy beans for dinner tonight. I hope that is okay with you?"

"You know you don't always have to cook, Aunt Venus, I can do the cooking."

"I love to cook, love, and my Gerald, loves my cooking, he would have a fit if someone else cooked for him. He always believes that someone is trying to poison him," she snickered.

Tori failed to find the joke in the statement and focused on the cluster of weeds before her.

By six pm the ladies had done half a quarter of the patch that Gerald had assigned to Venus. Tori got up and assisted Venus to her feet. "Lets' freshen up and have some supper. My Gerald said he would come in a little later this evening to take a shower. He has asked me to give him a haircut. His hair is as long as Rapunzel's," She chuckled. "Only his is silver and hers was gold," she said, cracking into laughter again.

It was around nine in the evening when Tori felt a soft knock on her door.

"Come in."

It was Venus. "Hon, I seem to have misplaced the clippers I use to shave my Gerald. I have searched everywhere, and I can't find them. I thought maybe if you could lend a hand in searching with me, maybe we might find them before he gets out of the shower?"

"Sure, sure," Tori whispered.

As they searched the house top to bottom, Tori couldn't help but feel acutely uncomfortable being at the home of a man she had never, not even once, seen in person, let alone greeted. She was in the kitchen, pulling every drawer, opening every door in search of the silver clippers Venus had described. Pixie was up to her feisty self, barking up a storm, putting Venus on edge.

"Let me check on top of the fridge, maybe," Tori announced.

"Oh, don't look on top of the fridge, there is so much dust up there you could make another Adam," Venus said in a shaky voice.

Tori noticed that this evening Venus was a little shaky. Was it the fact that her Gerald was in the house? Or was it the fact that she was there, while her Gerald was in the house? Tori wondered.

"Love," Venus whispered. "I think my Gerald might have left them in the nursery, a couple of months ago he tried to shave and almost lobbed off his right ear," Venus lowered her voice even more, "Do you mind just quickly nipping over there and having a quick look before he comes out from the shower. I don't want to put him on edge," Venus' eyes glistened with tears.

"Sure, let me dash there quickly," Tori said, exchanging her slippers for crocs.

It was dusk. There was still enough sunlight for her to make her way to the shed Venus referred to as her Gerald's nursery. She had never been in the nursery, so she was not sure what to expect. The door creaked as she gently opened it. She was greeted by a strong sterile smell. Her eyes adjusted to the bright lights in the nursery, noticing the immaculate upkeep of the lab. "This is no nursery," Tori whispered to herself, as she walked cautiously through Gerald's haven. She scanned the surfaces in search of the clippers. All she saw were syringes and jars with decapitated pieces she assumed were from animals. Guns were hanging across one of the back walls, and scientific books were on yet another wall. "This is definitely not a nursery," she whispered again, "It's a mad scientist lair."

An inaudible video was playing on loop. A man was explaining something. A graph popped up on the screen, "Culturing viruses in a lab," Tori walked up to the laptop and unmuted. The man gave a condensed explanation of how one can multiply a virus in a lab. Her eyes darted to the papers that were scattered around the laptop. There was a book on Rinderpest (also cattle plague or steppe murrain), which explained it as an infectious viral disease of cattle, domestic buffalo, and many other species of even-toed ungulates, including gaurs, buffaloes…" Tori's mouth went dry. "This is what Glen was talking about," she whispered to herself. "I need to take pictures," she searched her pocket and realized she left her phone in her room. "Rats!" Tori scanned the room again in search of what she had been sent for and located the clippers; she picked them up quickly and rushed back to the house.

Venus had been waiting by the front door. "What took you so long," she whispered angrily.

"Sorry, it was hard to locate them," Tori mumbled.

"Thank you for getting them; he just came out of the shower. You can stay in your room till I am finished cutting his hair. He is insisting on spending the night in his nursery," Venus muttered.

"Okay, I will be in my room," she murmured as she followed Venus back into the house, and slid into the guest room as Venus walked into her bedroom. Tori waited a while, the couple chatting quietly before Tori heard the clippers come to life as Venus started to shave her husband's hair. Tori knew she had to act quickly. She clawed through her purse and found her phone, put it on silent, and moved softly to the supposed nursery. As fast as she could, she started to take pictures of everything she could lay her eyes on, from the glass jars to the paperwork that Gerald had printed out; she took pictures of his handwritten notes, the whiteboard with strange formulas, temperatures, times and dates she couldn't make out. There was a notebook, Tori started to slowly page through it. There were pictures of buffalo, drawings, and graphs of different viruses. It seemed to Tori that the man had tried different types of viruses before settling for the Rinderpest. As she kept paging through she found a picture stuck in between the pages, it was the same picture she had seen on the wall in the house, the picture of their son, the one that had been killed by a buffalo.

"Glen needs to see this," she breathed, as she tapped on her phone.

As Tori turned to walk out of the nursery a shadow towered over her, then suddenly everything went pitch black.

Sedudu Island

As Tori came to, she could hear the loud noise of a rudder as if she were on a boat. Her head was throbbing; she tried to feel the back of her head but found her hands were bound together. As she wiggled, she realized her legs had shackles on them too. It was dark, but the moon was out, so one could decipher shadows shifting in the night. Screaming was of no use as she had been muzzled.

"Ahhhh, she is up!" a stale voice announced. "I was wondering when you would come to. You know, I don't like people poking around in my," he paused then whispered, "nursery," the man said in a sinister tone. "Especially people I have shown hospitality to. You have been staying at my place, no? Eating my food, breathing my air, using my water, talking to my wife, sitting on my couch, no? I have been watching you," he spoke deliberately slowly, as though each word that came out of his mouth had been carefully selected and carved. "You think I don't know who you are, Miss Amin," he paused and then tilted his head slowly. The act was so strange it reminded Tori of a psychotic doll in a thriller she once saw.

Tori's pulse quickened as she realized where she was. Out on the Chobe with the mad hatter, Venus called a husband. The night was still. Tori could not hear any other boats around, only the noise coming from Gerald's boat.

"You know it's illegal to drive into the Chobe at this hour," Gerald grinned. "I don't normally do this, but I thought for you, Miss Amin, I would make an exception. I mean, how often does one get a private tour at this hour. You must count yourself privileged,"

Gerald touched the top of his cap and bobbed his head at Tori.

Tori tried to make a sound.

"What is that, ma'am? You want to know where we are going, don't you?" he said, wiggling his crooked finger. "Well, I have a few friends that live on Sedudu Island that I would like to introduce you to."

Tori tried to get herself loose, but every time she tried, the rope would cut into her flesh.

"You can't get loose, miss, I learned how to tie a rope from the Bushmen. You might have seen my pictures on our wall as you were snooping around our house. And you saw our Peter. He was twenty when that cruel creature killed him. TWENTY! He screamed before going into a hush. "And so now it is payback. I have finally found the right thing to eliminate the Cape buffalo from our lives. No parent will ever have to be told a buffalo has dismembered their child. No one. I will make sure of that. It's a virus you know." The man continued. Aimed specifically at those beasts, I took much care. Botswana should thank me really." The boat suddenly went quiet. Gerald smiled. "We have arrived ma'am. Did you know that when young crocodiles hatch they have a length of twenty to thirty centimeters? Mhm, interesting fact neh. And during the first three to four years these critters increase in length by about 30 centimeters per year. A Nile crocodile is actually really impressive. Its body length is about a meter to three meters long when found in sub-Saharan countries, here in the Chobe, they can grow to about five to six meters in length. The crocodiles in the Chobe are one of the largest in the world, weighing in over a ton. There are different types of croc you know Miss Amin, you have Saltwater, the Marsh, the Dwarf, Cuban, Crocodylus with the pointed snout, the Siamese, the Mugger… and many more… But do you know which crocodiles we find here in the Chobe Miss Amin?" he paused, stretching his neck as though listening to Tori's response. "That's right, The Nile."

There was movement in the water; Tori shuddered at the thought of being eaten alive by an apex predator. Hippos could be heard "laughing" in the distance. On any other night, the scenery would have been magical. However, with Gerald in full mad form, Tori was instead scurrying for ideas on how she was going to escape.

The boat came to a dead stop near a patch of land.

"Sedudu Island" Gerald announced as he walked to a cooler box that was tucked away under an industrial plastic sheet. "Did you know there was a dispute between Botswana and Namibia," Gerald started as he took off the lid from the cooler box. He scooped out a dead fish and flung it into the water. "Years ago the two nations wanted to claim the island as their own, Botswana eventually won the dispute." Gerald scooped what Tori assumed was bloody fish water from the cooler and threw it into the murky waters. "Our guests should be making their way over in a minute," Gerald nodded. "Yes, Sedudu. Namibia wanted it, and Botswana was like no, no, it is ours. So eventually both governments agreed to submit their claims for sovereignty of the island to the International Court of Justice."

Tori wriggled in her attempt to try and get loose.

"What was that? How did the dispute get resolved? Was that your question?" Gerald tilted his head giving Tori his left ear. "Well, since you asked so politely, let us go back to 1890. You see, when eastern boundaries of the Caprivi Strip along the Chobe were defined in the Berlin Treaty of 1890, they were vague as to where the middle of the main channel was in the Chobe."

Gerald was so engrossed in his historic narration that he was completely oblivious that Tori had been able to set her hands loose. She had found a sharp object which she presumed to be a harpoon on the floor just behind where she sat.

"Kasikili Island as the Namibs call it then needed to be measured. The bed profile was taken, the depth and width as well as the volumes of water flowing within the two channels," Gerald pointed. "The northern channel, as well as the southern side, were all measured during different seasons in order to get an accurate reading. Eventually, the court ruled in favour of Botswana. The northern side of Sedudu/Kasikili Island being considered or determined as the main channel, the northern channel, is this one," he pointed to the channel that was on the Botswana side. "And that is how the dispute was resolved," he nodded. "Interesting isn't it?"

Tori nodded as she tried to forge a plan forward.

"I think that was enough time to allow our friends time to make their way to our boat. Time they were served the main course."

As Gerald stood up to walk towards Tori, an angry hippo charged for the boat. Gerald scurried to the front of the boat to try and restart it, but before he could reach the ignition, the boat had capsized. Tori held her breath as she wriggled her feet free praying fervently that she would not become hippo fodder. When her head finally popped back up she found she was under the boat. She tried to keep as still as she possibly could so as not to draw attention to herself. She could hear screaming and assumed it was Gerald. A few shots were heard and then silence. Tori breathed heavily under the boat; she prayed it would not start to sink, sending her to the depths of the waters that Gerald had just educated her about. Muffled voices could be heard. Tori thought she was losing her mind, but the voices could be heard louder and louder. The water under her was starting to get agitated.

"Helloooooo?" a voice was calling.

Tori was quiet, afraid it was Gerald.

"National Defence Force Hello?" the voice announced again.

Tori almost choked on the water under her, "Hello! She screamed, trying her best not to move underwater. "HELP!"

A few minutes passed before she felt something pull her at her legs, she fought vigorously, screaming in between gulps, the terror of being drowned by a Leviathan had taken over her, she punched, and kicked violently in attempts to free herself. A few seconds later she found herself kicking and punching the air.

Qorokwe Concession

IT HAD BEEN TWO MONTHS SINCE her Sedudu Island ordeal. Tori sat by the edge of the infinity pool attempting to read Deception Point by Dan Brown. She had read the opening couple of lines about a dozen times before she decided to put the book down. The scars on her wrists and ankles were still visible. As she closed her eyes she could still hear Gerald's voice whispering in her ear. She had had night terrors since that time when she had been fished out of the croc infected Chobe River by the BDF team that had been on patrol for poachers that formidable night.

There had been rumours of an impending lockdown due to the CoronaVirus. Sixty nine cases had been reported in South Africa, people were growing weary of the Chinese people in their communities. America was leading in the number of infections with England right on its tail. Tori was worried about the tourism business. If a lockdown was to occur, that would mean no tourists coming into Kasane. It would not only affect her business but the entire country's economy.

"Are you ready for your game drive ma'am?" Arnold, the guide assigned to Tori, nudged.

"Yes Arnold," Tori smiled sheepishly. She gathered her bag and followed Arnold to the jeep. A couple in their sixties sat on the seats just behind the driver's seat. Tori smiled and kindly greeted them before jumping to the back.

"We have one more guest joining us before we can head off," Arnold announced. "Which animal are you hoping to see?" he asked.

"Leopard," the couple cried out.

"And you miss Tori?"

"I am just happy to be on the drive," she smiled.

"Oh, there is our guest," Arnold said as he turned on the ignition.

The man jumped into the jeep and immediately planted himself at the back with Tori. Tori who had been tinkering with her camera, did not take note of him.

"Hey Tori, it is you is it not?"

Tori lifted her eyes and tilted her head to find Gabe right next to her. She smiled, "What are you doing here?"

Gabe smiled back. "Well, I guess you must have heard of the lockdown. I am travelling back to Austria with the repatriation flight from Joburg soon. But before going back I thought I should give myself a little treat."

"Nice."

"And you, why are you here?"

Tori made a face, where do I even start. "It's a little retreat for me. I had a bad experience and had to get away a bit."

"Oh?"

"Yah, remember that buffalo case in The Chobe?"

"Yes, it turned out that some nut was killing the buffalo or something like that."

"Mmm, and that nut was the husband of a friend of mine. He got killed by a hippo while he was trying to feed me to the crocs."

"What!"

"Yah. I found out he was the one that was behind all the killings. He knocked me out, and the next minute I was tied up in a boat in the middle of the night on our way to Sedudu Island."

Gabe could not believe what he was hearing.

"How did you find out he was the one that was killing the buffalo?"

"Venus, his wife had agreed to accommodate me at her place because all the lofts at Peter's Place were fully booked. So I stumbled across his secret lair. While I was collecting evidence, he knocked me over and tied me up."

"How did you get free?"

"Divine intervention I would say."

"No, but really," Gabe looked intensely concerned.

"The BDF were doing their rounds that evening, and they found me under the boat. An angry hippo had capsized the boat where I had been with Gerald, chopped him to pieces, and went on its merry way. I stayed motionless under the boat praying that the crocs didn't get me."

"My goodness, that sounds horrendous."

"I can hardly sleep."

"I can imagine."

"So this is my little getaway before the lockdown is announced."

"Well, I am glad you are here. Not glad why you are here. Cause that is a spine-chilling story, but glad you are here," he said, patting Tori's left hand that had been resting on her knee.

Arnold had taken a totally different route from the one they had taken when she had been with Mpho, Glen, and Mark. They were on the far end of the concession. Suddenly the landscape changed from mopane trees, shrubs, and acacia trees to long lush green grass. There was another tour group in front of them. Arnold spoke into his walkie talkie. He approached the other group cautiously. "Lions," he announced.

As their jeep approached an insignificant shrub they noticed two male lions lying under the shade.

"Tripod and Quad," Arnold announced.

"Why do you call them that?" The old lady asked as she took out her camera to take a few pictures.

"Tripod was involved in a territorial battle and ended up with a partially dislocated hind leg, hence his name Tripod, referring to his three normal legs. Quad, his most trusted companion has all his four legs intact with no abnormalities," Arnold answered.

"Interesting," the old man said, afraid to move a muscle.

The vehicle was so close to the man-eaters, that one could brush their mane, should one be brave enough and confident enough that the limb would still be unscathed afterward.

"What happened to his wife?" Gabe had switched his attention back to Tori.

"Still in Kasane."

"Yah?"

"Mmm, those two had a strange relationship. It's like they were constant ships in the night."

"Mmm, that is strange."

"I think the relationship was strained when they lost their son years back. That is the reason why Gerald had a grudge against the buffalo. It killed his eldest son."

Gabe made a quizzical face. "People lose relatives all the time to wild animals, but don't go on an assault like what this Gerald did."

"Yah, he was unstable waitse. Very unstable. Even the way he was speaking to me, I could tell that a few wires were crossed."

"Mmm."

"Yah."

The tour carried on with Arnold pointing out every bird he could spot. The old lady in front had a bird book on hand, and each time Arnold announced a bird sighting she would page through the book to try and locate the bird and read up on it.

"What happened to you that time?"

"When?"

"At Cresta Mowana, you just up and left while we were in the middle of a conversation."

"Oh, my boss walked in."

"So?"

"I don't like drinking at the same place as my boss. Once he spots you, you will never be able to enjoy work again, he will make churlish comments in front of your coworkers, always referring to the time he spotted you having a beer or a cocktail."

"That is very petty."

"Tell him that," Gabe chuckled.

"So are you planning to come back?" Tori asked.

"It's hard to say."

"Mmhm."

"So", Gabe trod lightly. "You and Glen?"

Tori smiled. "There was never a me and Glen. I may have thought something would materialize there, but it never did."

"Oh?"

"Yah, he is with a good friend of mine now,"

"But your good friend is already married?"

"A new friend, Billie-Jean."

"Oh, okay. And you are…"

"Not dating."

"If I were to ask you out again would you run?"

"I must say you picked your moment well, where would I run to without risking getting ripped to shreds by lions," Tori giggled.

Gabe's eyes prodded for an answer.

Tori played with her hair as she looked for the right words. "You are leaving. What would be the point of us courting?"

"Video conferencing is available."

A little smirk tickled the edge of Tori's lip. "I don't believe in long-distance relationships. That won't work for me."

Gabe gave off a satisfactory smile.

"What?"

"You just acknowledged that you wouldn't mind us dating."

"Well. I don't know how it would work with you all the way in Austria."

"I will be back soon."

"Yah?"

"Yah. My mother is not exactly a spring chicken, so I would rather be there for them should this virus drag on."

"Very noble of you," Tori nodded, impressed at the reason for Gabe's return to Austria.

"So should I ever find myself in Botswana again, where can one find you?"

Tori smiled. "Meet me in Kasane."